D1527123

# DR STANTONS EPILOGUE

T L SWAN

# ALSO BY T L SWAN

My Temptation (Kingston Lane #1)

The Stopover (The Miles High Club #1)

The Takeover (The Miles High Club #2)

The Casanova (The Miles High Club #3)

The Do-over (The Miles High Club #4)

Miles Ever After (The Miles High Club – Extended Epilogue)

Mr. Masters (The Mr. Series #1)

Mr. Spencer (The Mr. Series #2)

Mr. Garcia (The Mr. Series #3)

Our Way (Standalone Book)

Play Along (Standalone Book)

The Italian (The Italians #1)

Ferrara (The Italians #2)

Stanton Adore (Stanton Series #1)

Stanton Unconditional (Stanton Series #2)

Stanton Completely (Stanton Series #3)

Stanton Bliss (Stanton Series #4)

Marx Girl (Stanton Series – set 5 years later)

Gym Junkie (Stanton Series – set 7 years later)

Dr. Stanton (Dr. Stanton – set 10 years later)

Dr. Stantons – The Epilogue (Dr. Stanton – epilogue)

# GRATITUDE

*The quality of being thankful;*
*readiness to show appreciation for, and to return kindness.*

# DEDICATION

*I would like to dedicate this book to the alphabet.*
*For those twenty-six letters have changed my life.*
*Within those twenty-six letters, I found myself*
*and live my dream.*
*Next time you say the alphabet remember its power.*
*I do every day.*

# DR STANTONS EPILOGUE

# CHAPTER 1

Cameron

**Two weeks earlier**

ASHLEY SMILES into her cocktail glass as she sits across the table from me, and I feel myself melt.

This woman will be the death of me. No matter how long I look at her each day, it's never enough.

"Are we having dessert?" she asks as she opens the menu.

"You're my dessert," I reply as I watch her.

She smiles and raises a sexy eyebrow as she peruses the offerings.

It's Friday night—date night—and she's all mine. It's been a long week. I lost a patient in surgery on Tuesday and, as always, Ash was there to pick up my pieces.

I don't know what I would do without her. I can hardly

remember what it was like before she and Owen came into my life.

It must have been lonely, because they're my whole world now.

"Hmm, that's me. Sticky date pudding with butterscotch sauce." She smiles.

"Sticky date pudding sounds really, really good," I reply.

Her eyes rise to meet mine, and she smirks.

"Let's go home and have sticky date pudding?" I whisper.

She sips her drink and smirks against the glass. "Can I have yours?"

I chuckle. "Absolutely not."

She bites her bottom lip to stifle her cheeky smile, and reopens the menu. "My sticky date is off the menu, Cameron."

I rub my foot up her shinbone. "Until I say it isn't."

Our eyes lock and the chemistry buzzes between us. She smiles and looks back to the menu again. "Oh, this sounds good." She points as she reads. "Creamy ricotta and zesty lemon curd with a drizzle of cream through rich cannoli pastry."

"Hmm, yes." I frown. "That's me." I smile. "I do love to lick up cream that drizzles."

Ashley smirks over her menu. "Because you're an animal."

I pick up my wine glass and smile into it as I wink her way.

She smiles sexily and raises her glass to me.

"Bien que rien ne soit aussi bon que ta sève" I smile.

*Translation: Although nothing tastes as good as your cream.*

"J'en ai pour toi juste ici, bébé."

she whispers darkly.

*Translation: I've got some for you right here, baby.*

My cock starts to tingle. I can't handle it when she talks dirty to me. As soon as she begins, it's all over. "Let's go home."

"Let's not." She smiles as she takes my hand in hers over the table and kisses it. "I get you to myself one night a week and we always rush home to have sex because we can't get enough of each other."

I smirk. "You say that like it's a bad thing."

She slides my finger into her mouth and sucks on it, and I nearly convulse on the spot as I watch her. My cock starts to thump. She sucks my finger again and her eyes close in pleasure. "Do you know how loved you are, Cameron?"

I get a lump in my throat, not because she's saying it but because I know it's true.

"I do," I whisper.

She smiles, and kisses my hand before she places it back on the table and holds it in hers.

*I do.*

*I do.*

I frown as I watch her peruse the menu again, and a strange feeling comes over me—one I've never had before.

I want to hear her say *I do*... to me.

I frown as the fog lifts, and suddenly my mind becomes crystal clear.

What am I waiting for?

She's the one. I know she's the one.

She glances up from her menu and smiles sexily. "What's wrong?" She asks.

I sip my wine. "What makes you think that there's something wrong?" I reply.

"You look like you just swallowed a fly."

I throw my head back and laugh. If only she knew what I was thinking about.

"You probably should stop swallowing bugs and put that big mouth of yours to good use under the table instead," she mutters dryly as she continues reading. "That's what you really should be doing."

I picture myself under the table going down on her, and I shuffle around in my chair to allow my cock some much-needed room. "Hurry up and order your dessert. You're getting fucked in the parking lot downstairs in approximately fifteen minutes."

She smiles darkly and licks her lips. "Make it ten."

———

We walk into the elevator and turn to the front. Three women and a middle-aged couple are behind us.

Ashley glances over at me and I smirk.

*Game on.*

"What time will your husband be home tonight?" I ask her out loud, so everyone can hear.

"I don't know, he's your father. You ask him," she replies flatly. She tilts her chin defiantly as she stares at the doors in front of her.

I keep my eyes facing forward as I try to keep a straight face. "I would, but I'm going to be balls-deep in his wife."

She drops her head and frowns as she tries desperately not to laugh.

"Oh, my fucking God," one of the girls behind us whispers as she elbows her friend.

"Listen." She glances over at me. "You can't tell your

brother about us. If he finds out I'm fucking you, too, it's not going to be pretty."

I drop my head and scrunch my eyes shut.

"What a slut," the girl whispers to her friend.

I turn to face the girl. "Do you mind not speaking about my father's wife, my brother's mistress, and my hot little fuck buddy like that?"

The three girls' eyes widen in horror, and Ashley puts her hand over her mouth and bursts out laughing. It's contagious and, unable to help it, I laugh, too. The doors open just in time and I grab her hand and pull her out into the parking lot.

We begin to walk to the back corner where our car is parked. "That was a bad one." She laughs. "Your father and your brother." She shakes her head. "Where do you come up with this stuff?"

"You started the father." I laugh as I grab her ass. "My brother was an added bonus."

I push the key lock and the lights flick on my Aston Martin. Ash goes to the passenger side and I follow her and quickly pin her against my car.

We kiss, and her hands rise up my neck and into my hair. We kiss again and again, and God, this woman makes me crazy. I unzip my suit pants and she frowns as she looks down at me. "I wasn't joking about fucking you in my car," I growl.

Her eyes widen, and she glances around the car park. It's semi-dark and nobody is around.

"Here?" she whispers.

"Right here." I get into the passenger side and push the seat back as far as it will go.

Ashley looks around the parking lot guiltily.

"Get the fuck on my cock now," I growl.

She bubbles up a giggle as she hitches up her dress a little. "You are a cream-licking deviant, Dr. Stanton," she whispers as she falls into a straddle position above me and slowly closes the door behind her.

I pull her panties to the side and swipe my fingers through her flesh.

She's burning hot and dripping wet. "Yes," I hiss. Hmm. "Fuck, you feel good." I slide my cock back and forth through her lips and pull her down onto me in one hard slam.

Her mouth goes into a perfect 'O' shape and she closes her eyes. She holds the head rest behind me with both hands.

It's magnified in this small space... the feeling of her. The feelings I have for her.

Our mouths clash together in desperate need. "Bring your legs up," I push out.

She struggles a bit. "The damn gear stick is in my way." She hits her knee hard. "Ouch!" she yells. "If you're going to fuck me behind your father's and brother's backs, can you at least buy a panel van?"

I laugh out loud and grab her hipbones. "Done." I pick her up and slam her back onto me.

"You're a very bad man, Cameron Stanton," she breathes above me.

"And you are an excellent stepmother."

———

It's Wednesday afternoon and I'm just arriving at Joshua's and Adrian's office.

I have news, and I asked them to keep the afternoon free for me.

"Hey." I smile as I walk into Joshua's office.

Murph is on his laptop on the couch with papers scattered all around him, and Joshua is standing by the window with a golf putter, putting a golf ball into a little fake hole thing.

"Working hard, I see," I mutter to Joshua.

I slap Murph's hand in greeting.

"Fuck off, this is how I think," Joshua replies, distracted. He slowly hits the golf ball and it misses the hole by a mile.

"You are the worst golfer I've ever seen," I tell him.

"I know, right?" Murph rolls his eyes.

"I'd like to see you do better," Joshua replies.

"I would, but I'm too busy working," Adrian says, deadpan.

"You ready to go?" I ask.

"Yeah." Joshua frowns. "What are we doing again?"

I inhale deeply as I brace myself to say this out loud. "We're buying Ashley an engagement ring."

Adrian's eyes widen in excitement. "Oh, my God!" he shrieks as he jumps from the couch. Joshua breaks into a broad smile and slaps me hard on the back before he shakes my hand. "Congratulations, mate." He laughs.

"Well, that's premature." Adrian smiles as he pulls me into an embrace. "She didn't say yes yet."

My eyes widen as nerves dance around in my stomach. "She will say yes, won't she?" I frown in horror. The thought that she might say no hadn't even crossed my mind.

"I wouldn't if I were her," Joshua jokes as he grabs his wallet and keys. "Imagine being fucking stuck with you for life."

"You two are," I reply as I fix my hair in my reflection in the window.

He rolls my eyes. "I know. You annoy us daily."

Adrian laughs and puts his hands up to his face. "Oh my God, what ring are we getting?"

I shrug.

"Well, what shape does she like?"

I shrug again. "I don't know. There are shapes?"

"Well, what kind of diamond are we getting?" He frowns, agitated.

"I don't fucking know, do I? What is there?"

Joshua closes his eyes and pinches the bridge of his nose. "Give Murph your credit card, and you and I will go to the pub for the afternoon. I'm sensing this is going to be hell."

"Tempting." I smirk. "Nope, I'm doing this right. And we need to think of a way for me to pop the question."

Adrian narrows his eyes as he thinks. "Yes, it definitely has to be perfect."

"Remember those fucking lights you had me stringing up for hours, Stan?" I ask as I open the door for us to leave.

He smiles. "They worked." We walk out through the doors.

"Yes, fairy lights are the only reason Natasha said yes," Adrian mutters dryly. "You two are so stupid."

"We're going shopping for the afternoon," Joshua tells the two bodyguards who are waiting by the door. "Have the cars follow us at a distance today, please."

"Of course, sir," the bodyguard replies as he gets on the phone to the other guards downstairs.

"I'm driving," I say, and we walk out and get into the elevator.

"You brought the Audi?" Adrian asks in surprise.

"Yep."

"But... you don't have Owen."

I shrug happily. "I'm a family man now. I don't need to drive a flashy car anymore."

Joshua smirks. "Who are you and what have you done with my brother?"

———

We walk into the hundredth jewelry store in four hours, and I exhale deeply. Murph and Joshua peer into the cabinets while I walk around with my three gift bags safely in my hand.

I haven't found Ash an engagement ring yet, but I have bought her a pair of diamond earrings, a bracelet with a diamond 'O' pendant, and I got Jenna a necklace for taking such good care of Owen.

I never bought a girl jewelry before. It's kind of fun, to be honest.

"Look, will you fucking concentrate?" Joshua snaps. "This is the last shop we're looking at today. I want to go home. I've had enough of this shit."

"Hmm..." I hum as I look around.

"Just find the style you like and then we'll get one made. I think that's the best idea," Joshua suggests.

"What about this one?" Adrian points to a square-cut diamond ring.

"Yeah." I purse my lips as I think. "I like the round ones."

Adrian narrows his eyes. "Ashley wears rose gold, right?"

"I don't know, it's a different colour kind of thing."

"Yes, she wears rose gold," Joshua replies as he looks through the glass cabinet. "Her watch is rose gold."

"How do you know about rose gold?" I frown.

"Because I looked for that ring of Natasha's for ages before I found it, and now I know everything there is to know about everything."

Adrian rolls his eyes. "Except how to get a golf ball in a hole."

Joshua's eyes flicker to Adrian. "I do know how to put golf balls in smart asses' mouths until they choke," he offers dryly.

"He'd like that. I'm sure it wouldn't be the first ball he's had in his mouth," I mutter, distracted.

Adrian smirks.

We all continue to peruse the cabinets.

"Where should I ask her?" I think out loud.

Adrian puts his hands up, all animated. "Something so romantic that she'll be swept off her feet."

"Hmm."

"You can go to Kamala," Joshua suggests.

I cringe. "No, that's your place."

Adrian looks through the glass. "Why don't you fly her somewhere exotic?"

I curl my lip. "I want something sentimental." I narrow my eyes. "Something that only she will get."

"Eiffel Tower?" Joshua raises his eyebrows. "You two do speak French to each other all the time like total wankers."

I smile. "That could be cool."

"Oh, what about New York in the library where you showed her the newspaper advertisement." Adrian smiles.

"That's a good one."

"Why don't you just put an advertisement in the paper?" Joshua shrugs.

I put my hands into my pockets as I think. New York reminds me of when she didn't come home that night.

New York is forever ruined for me now. I feel my stomach churn at the horrible memory.

"Fuck this. Let's go to the pub." Joshua sighs.

"We'll do some research and come back," Adrian adds.

I nod. "Yeah, she might be getting a ring out of a bubble gum machine at this point. I fucking hate this shit."

———

It's Tuesday and I have just picked up Owen from preschool on my way home from work, and we jump into the car. "How was your day, buddy?" I smile into the rearview mirror.

"Good," he replies as he looks out the window and we pull out into the traffic. "Can we have McDonald's for dinner?"

"No," I reply flatly. "I think we're having pasta or something."

Owen screws up his face. "I'm sick of home food."

I smirk as I weave in and out of the traffic. "Wait till you have to cook the shit," I mutter under my breath.

"Will Mom be home?" he asks.

"Aha." I see a travel agent and I pull over. After wracking my brain for a romantic proposal all weekend, I got nothing. I thoroughly deserve my rating of three in the romance sector. "Yes, she'll be home soon. She's not working late tonight," I answer.

"Can I have a bath with crayons tonight?"

"No. Those things are ridiculous." Owen got bath crayons that were supposed to be great fun for his birthday, but all they did was fuck up two upstairs baths and stain the fucking carpet in the hall. "I threw those silly things in the rubbish. Do you remember the mess they made?"

He rolls his eyes as he stares out the window. "Santa will bring me more, anyway," he mutters under his breath.

I smirk because he's got a snarky little attitude, just like his mom.

"Don't count on it, buddy," I say as I park the car. "I've got a hotline to Santa. He and I are tight." I cross my two fingers and hold them up for him to see.

We climb out of the car and I take his hand as we head into the travel agent's. The door has a bell over it and it rings to let them know of our arrival.

"Yes. Hello." The girl smiles as she comes from the back room.

"Hello." I smile. Shit. I glance down at motor mouth, who's staring intently up at us. Didn't think this through too well, did I? "I'm looking for somewhere to go for vacation around Christmas time," I lie.

"Sure. Somewhere kid-friendly?" She smiles.

Owen grins up at her and swings his arms excitedly.

Hmm, fuck's sake. "Yes, kid-friendly," I confirm.

"Well, Disneyland is always great. Have you been there?" She smiles down at Owen.

His eyes light up and he shakes his head. "No. Oh, can we go, Dad? Can we?"

"Hmm... I'll just take some brochures, if that's all right."

"Okay, sure, where do you want brochures for?"

I narrow my eyes as I glance down at Owen. "Somewhere..." I pause.

She smiles knowingly. "Did you see our globe at the front?" she asks Owen.

"Oh." He immediately goes over to the globe and starts to look at it intently.

"You don't want kid-friendly at all, do you?" she whispers.

"Definitely not," I whisper back.

"What do you want?"

"Romantic kick-ass proposal place."

She smiles broadly and puts her hand on her chest.

I look at her blankly. *I'm not asking you.* "Any suggestions?"

"I have heaps. Give me your email and I'll send you a list of destinations tomorrow."

"Great." I take out my wallet and am just taking out a business card when I hear a loud crash and bang, and I look up in horror. "Owen!" I call.

He stands still, eyes wide.

Fucking hell.

Owen has spun the globe so hard it has come off its stand and gone flying into the window, smashing into a hundred pieces.

His little face falls and his eyes fill with tears. "It's okay." I sigh. "It was just an accident."

He scrunches up his face and begins to cry in embarrassment.

"I'm so sorry," I mutter. "How much do I owe you for the globe?"

"I'm not really sure it can be replaced." She frowns in horror. "It was my boss', a present from his late wife."

"Oh, fuck." I sigh.

"I know," she whispers, wide-eyed and mortified.

My phone rings and the name Bloss lights up my screen. "Excuse me for a moment, please." I answer the call. "Hey, Bloss."

"Hi, Cam. I just got a call from a solicitor."

"Why?" I glance up to see the poor girl trying to pick up the pieces of the smashed globe. I pinch the bridge of my nose and close my eyes in horror. I'm going to have to book my trip through here now.

"They want to see me urgently and left a message on my phone," she says.

"What about?" I ask.

"I don't know. What do you think it is?"

I shrug. "I have no idea."

"Do you think it has something to do with the court proceedings you lodged?"

I shake my head. "No, babe. Text me the number and I'll ring them and find out."

"Oh, could you? I'm still at work."

"Yeah."

"Where are you?" She smiles.

"I'm with Owen, breaking shit." I sigh.

She laughs, thinking I'm joking. This is not a drill. We are literally breaking shit over here. "See you in about an hour."

"Bye," I reply.

After paying the poor girl what she thinks the globe is worth, and promising to book a trip for her trouble, we head home and I turn the television on for Owen so I can go into my office and call the solicitor. "Hello, Lanvin Solicitors," the receptionist answers.

"Yes, hello." I narrow my eyes. "I had a missed call today from you and I was wondering if you could let me know what it was concerning, please."

"Just a minute. What was the name?"

I scowl because I know she probably won't give me any information. "Ashley Tucker."

"Oh." She pauses, and I can hear her keyboard clicking.

"I'm her husband," I reply. Well... hopefully soon-to-be.

"Ah, yes. Here it is. We just need Mrs. Tucker to come into the office, please."

I frown. "Can I ask what it's in regard to?"

"She's been named in a will."

"Whose?" I frown.

"Gloria Newton."

I smile and close my eyes. Gloria... beautiful Gloria. I bet she left Ash her book collection.

"That's great. Can we come in next week sometime, please?"

"Sure. Monday afternoon?"

"What's your last appointment?" I ask.

"Five-thirty."

"Okay, Ashley will be in then. Thank you for your call."

I hang up and smile to myself. I'm glad Ashley didn't take that call. It's going to be a really nice surprise for her.

———

"So?" I hesitate as I watch Ash over our dinner table. "I was thinking of booking a trip for us."

"Yes. Disneyland," Owen spits in excitement.

Ash raises her eyebrows and continues to eat.

I jump up and grab the pile of brochures from the side table and hand them to her. "What do you think?" I ask. "You can pick anywhere."

She looks through them and exhales. "I just don't have time to go away, Cam. Next year we can do something." She takes the last mouthful of food from her plate.

"Next year?" I frown. I can't wait a fucking year. "You're entitled to holidays, you know."

She shakes her head. "I don't want to go away right now. I already live in a resort half the time." She gestures to the house around us. "We don't need to go away when we are very lucky where we are."

"Well, maybe we could do a weekend?"

"Cam, I have exams and work and a child and preschool and a million things I have to do every day. I'm sorry. I just don't have the time at the moment. You and Owen go away to Disneyland if you want." She smiles. "That would be nice to spend some alone time with just the two of you."

She stands and kisses my cheek before she takes the plates to the sink. "Thanks, though."

I scowl. How the hell am I supposed to think of some romantic fucking thing when she won't leave the house?

My score is dropping to one.

I look through the brochures as I wrack my brain.

Maybe I should ask her in an elevator. At least then if she said no I can pretend it was a skit.

She yawns. "I'm going to have a shower and then I am going to lie down on the couch and do nothing," she announces.

"Owen and I will wash the dishes." I sigh, preoccupied. The poor thing is exhausted. She works way too hard. I remember being an intern, and it was hell.

She disappears up the stairs and I flick through the brochures, scratching my head.

"Well, she doesn't want to go away, Owie." I sigh.

"She would go to Vegas."

My eyes glance to his in surprise. "Why would she go to Vegas?"

"Because that's her favorite place."

"Why is Vegas her favorite place?" I frown.

"Because that's where she met you and you gave her my seed."

I smile. "It is."

"She said that one day when she has enough money she's going to take me there."

"Did she, now?"

He smiles and then shakes his head, widening his eyes. "But I'm not giving any seeds out when I kiss girls."

I laugh out loud. "I should hope not, Owen Stanton. You're four!"

# CHAPTER 2

**Ashley**

My HEART BEATS FAST as Cam kisses me slowly while he pulls out of my body and rolls off me, falling onto the bed beside me.

"Hmm." He smiles happily. "Good morning, Miss Tucker."

I smile sleepily. "Why don't you wake me up like that every morning, Dr. Stanton?"

"Ask your son," he mutters dryly. "I'm quite sure he doesn't want to see parent porn before pre-school."

I giggle.

It's 5:00 a.m. and we have been blessed with a childfree morning. Owen slept in his bed all night long.

"Surgery today?" I ask.

He rubs his eyes sleepily. "Yeah, full day." He rolls to his side and kisses my temple as he puts his arm underneath my head. "What have you got going on today, Bloss?"

"I'm in ER." I sigh as I throw my leg over his.

He curls his lip in disgust. You have to be a special kind of person to work in ER. Cam and I are not those people. I mean, it's good in some ways. The experience is invaluable, but it's hectic and you never know what the hell is going to happen on your shift. Drug addicts, car accidents, stab wounds, police everywhere... there's usually something horrible going on. Nothing good ever happens in ER.

"What time do you finish?" he asks.

"Not until seven." I kiss his chest. "Do you mind if we give date night a miss tonight? By the time I get home, going out will be the last thing I'm going to feel like doing."

He kisses my forehead. "Pizza, wine, and hot bath it is."

"I love you." I smile.

He smirks and kisses my head. "What's not to love?"

I sit up and I push him back to the bed to lean over him. "That's not what you're supposed to say back, Cameron."

He smiles cheekily. "If I say it too much you'll get sick of hearing it."

I kiss his lips and my eyes search his. "I could never get sick of hearing you tell me you love me."

His eyes darken, and he suddenly flips me so that he's on top of my once again. In one slick movement he's managed to slide back in. "I think I'll take my tonight sex now, thanks." He bites my neck. "Tonight's looking sketchy."

I laugh as he flexes his dick inside me.

The door handle turns.

"Fucking leg alarm," Cameron whispers.

I giggle.

"Every time someone in this house is trying to get a fucking leg over, an alarm goes off and he appears from nowhere," he growls into my ear.

"Dad?" Owen calls. "The door's locked."

"Fuck it," Cameron whispers as he rolls off me.

I giggle and throw my nightgown on and open the door. "Good morning, my Owie."

He frowns with his hands on his hips. "Why was the door locked?"

"I'm not sure. I probably locked it by accident," I murmur as I go into the bathroom and turn the shower on.

Owen goes over to the bed. "Let me in."

Cameron pats the top of the bed. "Lie on top of the blankets, buddy. It's too hot underneath."

I smile as I hold my hand under the water. Little does he know his dad's a sticky, hot mess under those blankets.

Owen lies on top of the blankets and cuddles his father for a moment.

"Why don't you go and put your shows on, Owie?" I call. Cam needs to start getting ready.

"Yes, okay," Owen calls back before he jumps off the bed and runs downstairs.

I look around. Damn it. There are no towels in here. I walk down the hall to the linen press and when I return Cam is in my shower. I smirk at him and put my hand on my hip.

He likes the water cold.

I like the water hot.

Showers together when sex isn't included involve a lot of tap temperature changing by the both of us.

"You can have first shower," I mutter dryly.

He winks sexily. "Thanks, Bloss." He grabs the soap and starts to wash himself. "Don't mind if I do."

"You have three minutes," I call. I return to the bedroom, make the bed, and open the blinds. A minute later, Cam appears with my white towel wrapped around his waist. His broad chest and the six-pack bring a smile to my face.

I am one lucky bitch to get to wake up to this guy every day.

I get another towel from the linen press and hop into the shower.

Cam is shaving, and I watch him intently as I stand beneath the water.

He looks like a movie star in his white fluffy towel wrapped around him. He slowly slides the razor down his cheek as he concentrates. No matter how many times I watch him do this, it still fascinates me every time.

"So, I have a thing in Vegas in a few weeks," he says.

I pour shampoo into my hand. "Oh, okay."

"I thought you might want to come with me," he suggests casually as he glides the razor over his skin.

"When is it?" I ask.

He rinses his razor under the hot water. "I'm not sure. Couple of weeks? Over a weekend, I think."

I scrunch up my face at the thought of all the hassle of going somewhere, packing, socializing, unpacking... Ugh. Honestly, just getting through working full time and being a mom is exhausting enough. "No, that's okay, babe. You go and have fun. Owen and I will stay home."

His gaze switches to me as his razor glides down his face and he stops mid-air. "Well, no. I want you to come."

I scrub the shampoo around my head. "I'm not coming, Cam. How long are you going for?"

He rinses the razor under the water again. "Well, I *won't* be going if you two don't come," he snaps, annoyed.

"Stop being a baby." I rinse my hair. "You don't need me to hold your hand."

"You know, most women get excited when their boyfriend tries to take them away."

"I am excited. I'm just too busy." I reply.

He rolls his eyes and continues shaving in silence. "Your job is starting to piss me off," he mutters. "How can you be too tired to come away for a weekend? It's ridiculous."

I raise my eyebrows. "Excuse me?"

His jaw ticks in anger and he glares at me.

"Don't start pulling that crap, Cameron. I don't have three secretaries and ten interns running around after me at work all day. I'm one of the fucking runners! I don't stop from daylight till dusk. I'll go away when I want to go away." I get out of the shower and walk into the bedroom, wrapping the towel around my head. "Stop trying to tell me what to fucking do all the time."

*Spoiled brat.*

He continues shaving and I get dressed in a hurry before I make my way downstairs.

"What do you want for breakfast, Owen?" I call.

"Fruit Loops."

"You are not having Fruit Loops," I tell him firmly.

"Why not?" he fires back.

"Because they are not in a damn food group!" I yell. Fuck. The men in this house are infuriating today.

"Jeez. Settle down," he calls.

"Don't say that to me!" I shout. "Stop copying what your father says. You are not allowed to tell me to settle down. It's disrespectful."

I make his oatmeal and sit at the table with him and my cup of coffee. Five minutes later Dr. Stanton arrives down the stairs.

And I don't call him Dr. Stanton lightly, because as soon as he puts on that McDreamy suit the whole dynamic changes between us.

I'm instantly putty in his hand.

He walks past me, places his hand on my shoulder as a silent apology and I find myself smirking into my coffee.

"I hate oatmeal." Owen sighs.

"Owen. I don't know where this attitude is coming from about junk food, but the way you're going you're never getting it again."

He widens his eyes into his bowl and Cameron drops his head to hide his smile.

"But..." he begins.

"Owen. Don't talk back to your mother, just eat your breakfast now," Cameron cuts him off.

Owen drops his head and eats in silence.

Cameron makes his coffee and his morning protein shake then kisses my forehead. "I've got to run. See you tonight, Bloss."

"Bye, babe." I sigh as I blow out a breath. I grab his hand and pull him back to kiss him softly on the lips. He smirks and raises his eyebrow at my fiery behaviour this morning.

He kisses Owen. "See you tonight, buddy."

"Bye, Dad." Owen smiles up at him, and before I know it he's out the door. I hear his sporty Aston Martin take off down the driveway and the sound of the automatic gates open. I remember a time when I was just his intern and how exotic his two-hundred-thousand-dollar car seemed. Now that I know it's just a compact, flashy little thing that's really, really hard to have sex in, I'm totally unimpressed.

"Did you get out of the wrong side of the bed today, Momma?" Owen asks innocently.

I smirk and try to tame his wild hair with my fingers. "Maybe."

———

I stare at the angiogram report in front of me. It makes no sense. I'm in a cubicle with a man in his early thirties who has been brought into ER with a suspected heart attack.

He's scared, and he has every right to be.

His heart is not doing anything near what it's supposed to be doing.

"Peter, is it?" I smile sympathetically.

He nods way too fast, as if panicked, and he's having trouble catching his breath.

"It's okay. Calm down." I smile. "You're in safe hands now."

I read through the blood samples and go over the chest x-rays. I then go back over the electrocardiogram and the angiogram.

His results are not making any sense and I have no idea what's going on here. I need to call a specialist down.

"Peter, I'm going to call for a second opinion." I smile.

He nods. "Is something wrong?" He frowns.

I smile and pat his forearm. "Nothing that we can't take care of, don't worry. Try and get some sleep. I'll get a nurse to come and stay with you while I'm gone." I draw back the curtain. "Excuse me, Tammy," I say to the nurse who's making the bed next to me. "I need someone to stay with Peter while I just call upstairs, please."

"Sure." She smiles, walks in, and takes Peter's hand in hers. "I bet you're having an interesting day." She smiles.

Peter coughs as he tries to catch his breath, and nods.

I hot foot it to the phone and dial the cardiology wing. "Hello. This is Dr. Tucker in ER. Can I have a cardiologist come down here, please?"

"Sure thing. Where are you?"

"In E26."

"Okay, thank you. I'll send Jameson." She hangs up.

"Thank you," I say gratefully.

I walk back into Peter's cubicle to find he's having a panic attack.

"Peter. I need you to relax for me," I say as the nurse puts an oxygen mask on him. He pants heavily as he tries to breath.

*Fuck... hurry up, Jameson.*

Seb walks through ER and I dart out from the curtain. "Seb."

He turns. "Oh, hey, Ash."

"Can you help me for a moment, please?" I widen my eyes in a *help me I'm freaking out* way. He nods knowingly and follows me into the cubicle.

"This is Peter," I introduce them. "Peter was brought in by ambulance after collapsing at work."

"Hello, Peter." Seb smiles as he shakes his hand. I pass his chart and results to Seb, and I know that he can't actually do anything that I haven't done already, but I just want someone with me until help arrives. Seb knows what I'm doing, but goes through the chart anyway.

He frowns as he reads the results and his eyes flicker up to me.

"Jameson is on his way down." I smile as I try to act calm.

"Good," he mutters, distracted. "Do we have code blue prepared?"

"What's wrong?" Peter whispers in fear.

I smile. "Everything is fine, Peter. Stay calm for me." Two nurses come in and fuss about, sensing the oncoming disaster.

Code blue is a resuscitation team. I've already put them on notice. "Yes, code blue is ready," I reply as my nerves begin to bounce in my stomach.

"Well, Peter..." Seb tries to change the subject to lighten the situation. "You should feel very privileged to have Dr. Tucker looking after you."

Peter nods as he breathes into his mask, glancing between us. "Are you two dating?" he whispers.

"Well, one day, when Dr. Tucker gets her senses about her and dumps her loser boyfriend, we will be."

Peter smiles and I grin, too.

The curtain is dragged back, and Cameron stands before us. He's in his dark blue operating scrubs and is obviously in between surgery.

My eyes widen with horror. Did he just hear that?

He glares at Seb and I swallow the lump in my throat. "Is that so?" he says coldly.

Shit. Yep. He heard it.

Perfect timing.

Seb withers and I begin to perspire.

"Hello. My name is Dr. Stanton." He picks up the chart and reads it as his jaw continually ticks. Eventually his eyes rise to Peter. "Tell me what happened to you today, sir."

Peter rattles off what happened, but Cameron is too busy reading his report. He turns the pages back and forth, and goes through the bloods and x-rays.

We all hold our breath as we wait for his prognosis. The two nurses stop what they are doing, too, as they wait. Cam takes Peter's pulse, frowns, and takes it again. Then his eyes fall to the nurse. "Arrange a transfer to the cardiac wing immediately."

"Yes, Dr. Stanton."

He looks at the chart again and frowns. "Call a code blue ahead, please."

My stomach drops. Cam thinks Peter's going to go into heart failure at any moment. My own heart starts to race.

Within thirty seconds the room is abuzz with nurses, and two porters arrive to wheel Peter up to the specialty wing.

"What's happening?" Peter whispers.

"It's okay, Peter. You're coming with me so I can keep an eye on you," Cameron reassures him as he takes his hand calmly. "I'm a little concerned with your results, but you're in safe hands."

Peter's face falls.

Seb sees that as his escape plan. "See you later," he whispers as he tries to make a get-away.

Cameron glares at him. "Not so fast." He growls. "In my office. Now!"

My eyes widen.

Cameron turns on his heels and follows Peter's bed up the hall. Seb widens his eyes and then follows him sheepishly.

Oh my God. Oh my God.

Shit. I look around in panic. What do I do?

For five minutes, I pace in the room as I try to think of a plan.

I grab a file and go to the nurse's station. "I just have to take this report upstairs," I lie.

"Sure thing."

I speed walk to the elevators and then up the two-mile corridor to Cameron's office.

I go to knock, but my hand freezes midair. I can hear Cameron yelling but I can't hear what Seb is saying in reply. Is Seb even saying anything?

What the fuck?

I put my head up to the door.

"Do I make myself fucking clear?" Cameron yells.

"Crystal," I hear Seb reply.

The door opens in a rush and I jump back. Cameron

appears, his cold eyes hold mine, and then he calmly walks down the hall towards Peter.

Seb appears and we both stand and watch Cameron disappear around the corner.

We glance at each other, and without a single word we both scurry back to work.

Well, that was awkward.

———

It's 5:00 p.m. I'm on my tea break, scrolling through my phone. I have a missed call from Natasha, so I call her back.

"Hey, Ash."

"Hello." I smile. "How are you? What's going on?"

"Well, Joshua just told me that you don't want to come to Vegas. Why not?"

I frown. "What... Vegas? Are you going?"

"Yes. The boys have a stag night and we thought that we could bring the kids and then have a night out for the girls."

I frown. Shit... I really don't want to go. "Yeah, I'm not keen." I sigh. "I'm just really busy right now, Tash. You go and have fun."

"Oh." She sighs. "I don't want to go without you. Why don't we bring Jenna?" she asks. "She could do with a weekend away, and there's plenty of room for her on the jet."

I scowl because, damn it, I know Jenna really does need a weekend away.

She would be so excited.

"Oh, we'll have so much fun and the three of us could go out on the Saturday night. My nannies are coming so the kids will all be fine," she continues.

I roll my eyes. "Yeah, let me think about it. I'm really not into it."

"Oh, please," she begs. "I desperately need a night out and Adrian is coming, too."

"Adrian is coming?" Hmm, it's getting tempting.

"Let me speak to Cam and I'll get back to you tomorrow." I sigh.

"Okay, babe. Please come." She hangs up and I shake my head.

I am so not going.

———

It's 9:00 p.m. and Cam isn't home from work yet. His secretary called me at 4:30 p.m. to let me know that he was held up in surgery. That's code for something is not going to plan. We stay at Cam's house three nights a week and then my house three nights so that Jenna can still care for Owen in the mornings and after-noons. Cameron would prefer to stay here all the time and get the nanny to work extra, but I feel that it's important for Owen to still spend as much time with Jenna as possible. Apart from me, she is the only other stable person who has been in his life since birth.

I've already retrieved Cameron's favorite red wine from the cellar in preparation for his bad day.

I didn't see Cam all day after he roasted Seb in his office, and I've just tucked Owen into bed. He's not happy that Dad's not home before bedtime. It seems surreal that just six months ago he never even knew who his father was.

I hear the automatic gates open and I smile and fill our heavy crystal glasses with the dark red. He must be exhausted after fifteen hours of surgery.

He comes in and walks into the laundry to take off his scrubs. "Hey," he calls as he heads straight up to shower.

"Hi," I call after him.

I wonder what happened to hold him up so late. I'll give him some time to unwind alone.

Ten minutes later he reappears in a pair of silk boxer shorts. "Hello, Miss Tucker."

I smile. He has that tone to his voice tonight—the deep *I'm about to fuck you really hard* tone.

"Hello." I smile as the butterflies dance in my stomach. They dance partly because I know he's pissed off about Seb and partly because I know he's had a shit day... but mostly because he looks off the charts fucking hot right now, half naked, standing here in the kitchen. My eyes drop down his torso to his rippled abdomen and the V of muscles that disappear into his silk shorts. My eyes rise to meet his.

He sips his wine and frowns in approval, licking his lips as he stares at his glass. "That's the stuff."

I smile and take a sip of my wine. "Was your day okay?"

He turns to the refrigerator and peers in.

"Your dinner is in the oven," I say.

"Thanks," he mutters as he takes it out and sets it on the counter. He pulls up a stool and takes a mouthful of the casserole. Our nanny, Madeline, prepared it for us, knowing that we were going to be late. She doesn't normally cook, as Cameron likes to, but she helps us out on occasion. He frowns as he chews and looks down at his plate. "What is this?"

I smile. I knew he wouldn't like it much. "Some kind of goulash."

"Hmm." He screws up his face and puts another mouthful into his mouth. "Interesting," he mutters.

I giggle as I watch him as he eats in silence. "What happened with Sebastian today?" I ask.

His eyes rise to mine, but he keeps eating until, eventually, he answers. "How long has he been flirting with you?"

"Seb is just being Seb, Cam. You know he doesn't mean anything by it."

"I don't like it."

I sip my wine. "What did you say to him, anyway?" I ask.

"Nothing that concerns you."

I frown. "Was it about me, Cam?"

"No. It was about him disrespecting me." He pauses for a moment. "And you."

I roll my eyes. "Don't roll your fucking eyes at me, Ashley. I won't stand for it." He snarls as he takes a bite of his food. "If he says one word out of line to you again, it's on."

"He knows we're together, Cam." I frown.

"And I know how much respect he has for other people's relationships." He growls.

I smile and rub my hand up his thigh. "You're kind of cute when you're jealous, you know."

He sips his wine. "I don't get jealous."

"Really?" I smirk,

He rolls his eyes and continues eating. "What is this food?" He grimaces.

I laugh because it really is bad. "You sound like Owen."

"Did he eat any of it?" He frowns.

I shake my head. "Nope. He ended up having toast."

"Don't blame him." He frowns as he chews. "Much safer option."

"So, Natasha called me today."

He nods and keeps eating. "What did she have to say?"

"You didn't tell me you were going to Vegas with them."

He shrugs. "Does it matter?" He sips his wine. "I should be the only person who matters enough to convince you to take a trip."

"Cam." I frown. "I'm just really tired."

He looks at me. "Why is that, Ash? Why are you so tired that you don't want to make any plans with me?"

I stare at him, and for some reason I get all emotional. My eyes tear up.

"It's not you," I whisper.

"Ash." His face falls. "What's wrong, baby?" he asks gently.

I shrug as I try to articulate my thoughts. "It's like..." I pause.

"It's like what?"

"It's like I had to be so brave and strong on my own for so long." I frown because I know this sounds ridiculous, even to me.

He frowns as he watches me.

I shrug. "Now that I have you to take half the load, my body has decided to relax and fall apart." I wipe a tear from my eye. "I feel weak, Cam. I feel tired and weak and could sleep for five years."

He smiles softly as he watches me.

"And I... I don't like it because *I'm* the one who holds shit together," I stammer.

He smiles and stands, and pulls me into an embrace. "You don't need to hold shit together anymore, Bloss." He kisses me softly on the lips. "I'm here to hold our shit together now."

I smile through my tears. "Promise?"

He kisses me softly and rubs his fingers down my cheek as he studies my face. "I promise."

I put my hands around his broad shoulders.

"Will you come to Vegas next weekend?" he whispers.

I smile. "If I must."

"Good." He kisses me softly. "Now, I know you're feeling weak, but luckily for you that's a great companion to how I'm feeling." He grabs my ass hard and I laugh out loud. "Now get up to our bed, on your hands and knees, because you are about to be fucked into next week."

I giggle and wipe my eyes. "Yes, Boss."

# CHAPTER 3

**Ashley**

I GLANCE over at Cameron as he drives. "Explain to me exactly what they said this appointment is about?" I frown. "Like, word for word."

"Nothing." He slides his hand up my thigh. "This is just a formality to finalize the changes to Owen's birth certificate."

I stare out through the front windscreen onto the rainy road. "Oh, okay."

He squeezes my thigh between his fingers. "It shouldn't take long, I don't think."

It's Monday afternoon and we're on our way to see the solicitor who called me last week. After tackling the traffic, we arrive and walk hand in hand to the office, through the swanky black doors.

The receptionist looks up from her computer. "Hello." She smiles and takes a double look at Cameron. "Ashley Tucker?"

I nod and swallow the nervous lump in my throat. Solicitors always make me jumpy.

"Take a seat, it won't be a moment. Can I get you a glass of water or a cup of coffee?"

"No, thanks." I fall into the seat and look around the office nervously. Cam takes my hand into his on his lap.

The office door opens and a kind-looking elderly lady smiles. "Ashley Tucker?"

"Yes." I stand nervously.

She holds her hand out to her office. "Just this way, dear." I grab Cam's hand for reassurance, and we walk in and take a seat at her large mahogany desk.

I clutch my purse tightly on my lap as she takes a seat opposite us. "Now. You know why we're here today?"

"The birth certificate?" I whisper.

Cam smiles broadly. "I didn't tell her why she's here."

My eyes flash to him in question.

The solicitor smiles broadly. "How lovely." She stands and takes a folder out of her large filing system. "Well, Ashley, you recently became friends with one of my clients."

I frown.

"Gloria."

My eyes widen.

"And Gloria has named you in her will."

I glance at Cameron and he smiles broadly. "You knew about this?"

He raises his cheeky eyebrows, and I shake my head. *What the hell?*

She takes out her large folder and opens it. "Gloria has left you her collection of Jane Austen books."

My mouth falls open and tears instantly fill my eyes. "Oh my God," I whisper. "Are you serious?" I scramble through my bag for a tissue. "That's amazing." I turn to Cam and he's grinning back at me. "Oh, that's so special to me. Thank you so much," I whisper. "When can we pick them up?"

She smiles as she watches me. "That's not all she left you, dear."

I frown.

"There's a property on three-hundred acres in San Diego, and a house in Burbank."

My eyes widen. "I beg your pardon?" The blood drains from my face.

She smiles and nods. "Yes, she left you everything that she owned."

My eyes tear up again and I look to Cameron, who's sitting there stunned.

"Are you serious?" I whisper.

"Completely." She shuffles through the paperwork. "I have some paperwork that you have to sign to make it legal."

I drop my head. "I was just her friend. Are you sure you have the right person?" I whisper.

"Positive. She was as smart as a whip and you made her last days wonderful. She contacted me six weeks before she died to arrange the details."

"Gloria..." I whisper.

Cameron drops his head as emotion takes over.

This is something else.

"Now, the house in San Diego hasn't been visited in ten years, so I have no idea what state it's in." She passes over a pile of paperwork with Xs marked where I have to sign. I start to make my way through them with signatures.

*Is this really happening?*

"And the house in Burbank was where she lived until she went into hospital, so everything inside it is yours, too."

I stare at her with the pen in my hand. "I can't believe this," I whisper.

I sign and sign and sign until I don't think my hand can take much more. Finally, forty-five minutes later, she hands me two sets of keys and the two title deeds.

I stare at the keys in my open hand then look up at Cameron, and he kisses me softly on the lips. "Congratulations, baby," he whispers.

"Cameron, this is too much."

"No, it's not." He smiles as he puts his arm around me and leads me out the door. "You deserved this because you loved Gloria."

"Cam, I wasn't her friend to get an inheritance."

He kisses me and smiles softly. "I know, but every day as I listened to you read *Pride and Prejudice* to her, I fell a little bit deeper in love with you."

I stare at him through my tears and he pulls me into an embrace. "Let's go home, Bloss." He chuckles. "Your house or mine?"


## Vegas

Cameron fusses around in Owen's bag. "So, you've got to take this bag tonight with you over to the other room when you stay there, Owen."

"Uh-huh," Own replies as he watches cartoons on television.

Cameron rubs his forehead as he thinks.

I smirk as I watch Cam dart around like a madman. Owen and I are lying on the queen bed, being completely lazy and unmotivated while Cameron is trying to organize us before he leaves for his stag night. It's 4:00 on Saturday afternoon, and we're in our luxury suite in Vegas. He's just about to go.

"Don't forget your blankie," he mutters almost to himself as he packs it in the bag.

He power-walks into the other room and then reappears, scratching his head. He mutters to himself and disappears again.

"Daddy's going cuckoo," I whisper as I snuggle into Owen.

Owen nods and continues to watch his shows.

"What time are you going out tonight?" Cam asks me as he appears again.

I shrug. "Don't know."

"Well, what are the plans?" He frowns.

I shrug again. "I don't know. There are no plans."

"No plans?" he repeats. "I thought you had plans." He walks over and checks the charge on Owen's iPad, plugging it in while he plays it. "What time did you say you would leave?"

"Oh, I don't care, we might just stay in bed. Might we, Owie?" I tickle Owen and he laughs as he tries to escape my clutches.

"Owen, don't forget to take your iPad tonight so you can play it if the other kids are on theirs," Cameron tells him.

"Okay. Can we get room service, Mom?" Owen asks excitedly.

"Let's get some milkshakes and fries." I smile.

"Yes." Owen punches the air.

"Ash, what time did Tash say that you're all going out?" Cam asks again as he puts his hands on his hips. "I would like to know what you're doing."

"I don't know." I frown. "Who cares? We'll get there when we get there."

He looks at me flatly.

"What's your problem?" I smirk. "Why are you so uptight today?"

"What? I'm not uptight. You're uptight." He disappears into the other room again.

I laugh. "Yes, that's why you've worn the carpet threadbare this morning with all your pacing."

"I'm not pacing," he calls out, annoyed.

He comes back in and stands at the end of the bed and watches me for a moment.

He's wearing his custom hunky jeans, a navy blazer, and a white shirt. His hair is in its usual style of dark, messy curls, and his beautiful square jaw shines in all its glory.

"You are one beautiful-looking man, Cameron Stanton." I smile.

He frowns and swallows a lump in his throat, his eyes searching mine. "You love me, right?"

"Yes."

"Like love, love? Like, serious shit love."

I smile. "As serious as love shit can get."

"Good. Good," he whispers to himself.

"Stop saying the naughty word, 'shit'!" Owen frowns as he plays on his iPad.

"Sorry," Cam splutters. "But don't you say it, either, please."

"Are you all right, Cam?" I ask.

"Yes. Why wouldn't I be?" He frowns.

"Because you look like you're about to throw up."

He runs his fingers through his hair and suddenly turns to leave like it's urgent. "Okay, I gotta go."

I stand to grab him in an embrace and he pulls away quickly. "Got to go, Bloss." He kisses me quickly and then kisses Owen. "See you tonight."

"Bye, Cam." I smile.

He heads for the door and then turns back. "Don't you want to know where I'm going tonight?" He frowns.

"Not really." I shrug. "Vegas, I assume.

"Witty," he replies dryly.

I smile and wink. "That's me. The witty witch."

He shakes his head and disappears out into the hallway, and I pick up the phone. "Hello, room service?"


## Cameron

It's just gone 7:00 p.m. and I'm at a bar with Joshua and Adrian. To go along with the stag night story, we had to pretend to be somewhere else. We've had a few drinks and I feel like I'm going to throw up.

"Will you relax?" Joshua smirks.

I drag my hand down my face. "She could say no, you know."

"She's not going to say no." Adrian rolls his eyes.

"Imagine that. I drop to my knee in a crowded club in front of everyone and she says fucking no." I frown as my stomach drops, and I tip my head back to drain my scotch from its glass.

Joshua laughs. "Would be kind of funny, though, right?"

"Hilarious," I reply deadpan.

Adrian chuckles.

"Seriously, this is bullshit. I've... I've felt sick since Wednesday," I stammer. "Maybe I'm not meant to get married." I shake my head as I feel perspiration heat my body. "Maybe this is the universe telling me this is a stupid fucking idea." I pinch the bridge of my nose and then I frown. "What if I fuck this up and she leaves me?" My eyes widen in horror. "Then I'll be divorced," I whisper in horror.

"Will you calm down? You're going to have a heart attack," Adrian replies.

"Why on earth would anyone get married more than once? This is absolute bullshit." I frown.

Joshua smirks into his glass. "I would never marry again."

"Really?" Adrian frowns.

"No." He thinks for a moment. "Natasha is it for me. If something happened to her I wouldn't do it again with someone else. She will be my only wife."

"You can't say that. Look at Nicholas," Adrian replies. "He said that, and he eventually got married again. Lucky bastard."

"Hmm." Joshua frowns. "Even if she wasn't here anymore I would be her husband."

My heart starts to beat hard in my chest. "Someone get me a fucking double scotch immediately. I can't deal with this shit."

Joshua laughs and stands to go to the bar.

"Show me the ring," Adrian asks.

I dig around in my pocket and pull out the black velvet box and open it.

It's rose gold with a three-carat, perfect white diamond sitting proudly. Adrian smiles broadly. "We did good finding this."

"I should hope so, it took a week. Do you think she'll like it?" I ask.

"She's going to love it."

"I would have liked a bigger one," I say as I study it.

"She wouldn't be able to wear it to work then," Adrian replies. "You want her to have something that she can wear all the time. Not just on special occasions."

I nod. "Yeah, I guess."

My phone dances across the table and the name Bloss lights up the screen. I smile and answer. "Hey, hot stuff."

"Oh, Cammy," she purrs.

Hmm. I glance up at Adrian and he frowns in question. She only calls me Cammy when she's drunk.

"I just rang to tell you that Vegas was a great idea."

"Are you drinking cocktails? How many drinks have you had?" I ask.

"Not many, but oh my God, I'm having the best time. The Amalfi Coasts here are amazeballs."

I put my hand over the phone. "Great. She's fucking plastered," I whisper.

Adrian puts his hand over his mouth in surprise and laughs.

"I love you," she slurs.

"Where are you, Bloss?" I ask.

"Oh." I hear her ask the others. "Where are we?"

"In the cocktail bar on level three," I hear Natasha's voice in the background. "Near the cute bartender."

I roll my eyes.

"On level three." Ashley hiccups. "The waiter is really cute, Cam."

I smirk. Oh, she's plastered all right. Ashley has a habit of pointing out good-looking men to me when she's drunk.

"Have a fun night," I reply.

I hear all the women giggle like stupid school girls. "Thank you for making me come to Vegas, Cam." She laughs. "This is, like, the best thing ever!"

I hang up and glance at my watch. "We still have four hours to go and she's drunk already!" I snap.

Joshua comes back to the table and places the six drinks on the tray on the table.

"Well, this is a fucking disaster," I grumble.

"What is?" Joshua frowns.

"The girls are hammered."

He glances at Adrian and they both burst out laughing.

"This isn't funny. I have four hours to go and she's drunk now. She won't make eleven o–fucking-clock. She'll be asleep in two hours from now."

Joshua sits on his stool. "At least if she says no she won't remember you asking." He sips his drink. "Less awkward."

"Fuck's sake," I whisper.

"Well, let's just bring it forward." Adrian frowns.

"No. It has to be at the same time at the same place as the first time we met."

They sip their drinks as they think.

"And I have the guy lined up to hit on her at eleven," I add.

Adrian rolls his eyes. "I'm pretty sure she's going to be hit on about fifty times before then. A hot chick like her doesn't have to ask for attention, especially if she's stupid drunk."

Joshua takes out his phone. "I'll ring Max." He dials the number, puts it on speaker, and sits in the middle of the table.

"Hey, boss," Max answers.

"What are the girls doing right now?" Josh asks.

"Sitting at the bar, drinking some sort of pink cocktail."

"They drunk?" Joshua frowns.

"Tipsy. The cocktail waiter is chatting with them as he makes them doubles."

Joshua's unimpressed eyes flicker to me, and Adrian laughs out loud.

"Great!" I snap. "This is just fucking great." I shake my head in disgust. "Where are you, Max?" I ask.

"Level three, cocktail bar."

"Okay, thanks, Max," Joshua replies flatly. "You have my permission to knock that cocktail waiter out."

"Roger that." He hangs up.

I drain my glass.

Joshua smirks as his eyes hold mine.

"Okay." Adrian holds up his hands. "I've got a plan."

Joshua rolls his eyes. "Here we go." He sighs.

"We pretend that we're walking through to the casino and we accidently bump into the girls. Joshua and I distract Ashley while you tell the other two to sober her up."

I narrow my eyes as I think.

"That's actually a good idea," Joshua replies. "She needs to eat something."

"Yes," Adrian urges. "Get the girls to take her to dinner and stop drinking for a little while, then it's all good." He holds up his hands. "Simple. Crisis averted."

"Fine!" I snap. "Finish these drinks and we'll go."

———

Fifteen minutes later, we walk into the cocktail bar the girls are in. We hear them before we see them. The three of them are sitting at the bar, laughing loudly, each with an exotic-looking pink cocktail in front of them.

Joshua and Adrian walk over to them and I slowly follow.

This was a bad idea. I should have just proposed at home in private. Why did I think this was a good idea? Yeah. I'm just going to do it another time.

The boys kiss the girls on the cheek as a greeting, and I stand back as I think.

Just at home with the two of us, no pressure.

I feel two hands slink around my waist and look down to see my beautiful girl smiling up at me. Her joy is infectious. "Hello." I smile.

She smiles goofily up at me. "Hello, my love."

My eyes hold hers, and in that instant moment my every fear dissipates.

I know this is right.

I love, Ashley. I will always love Ashley.

"Are you having a good time?" I kiss her softly on the lips.

"I am now that you're here."

I snake my hand around to her behind. "You're a terrible liar. I heard you laughing from the lobby."

She wraps her arms around my neck and nuzzles into my chest, and I widen my eyes at Natasha.

Natasha giggles and bites her bottom lip, sensing she's in trouble.

"Oh, Ash. Come and show me this drink you're having." Adrian distracts her as he holds up the cocktail menu.

I quickly walk over to Natasha and Jenna. "A word in private, you two," I whisper.

"Yes?" Natasha exclaims, too loud.

"Ssh!" I snap.

"I'm going to the bathroom," Jenna calls.

"Oh, me, too," Tash whispers guiltily.

Joshua chuckles and I roll my eyes. They're about as subtle as a Mack truck.

We walk around the corner, behind the potted plants, and I grab Natasha to stabilize her on her high heels. "What the hell are you doing?" I whisper. "Ashley's drunk."

Natasha's eyes widen in an over exaggerated way. "She is? We only had four drinks, though."

I glare at her. "And so are you!"

47

She totters on her heels as she tries to concentrate. "This is true. I think I could be. Oops." She points at me.

I roll my eyes and glance at my watch. "We still have three and a half hours. You need to sober her up."

"Yes," Jenna whispers. "We do." She starts to bounce up and down on the spot. "Oh, I'm so excited, I might die."

"Well, the two of you will definitely die if you don't sober her up immediately," I snap.

Natasha bubbles up a giggle and points to Jenna. "It's all her fault. The cute bartender was flirting with her and making our drinks super-strong."

Jenna laughs. "I need his number."

"Oh my God. You so do," Natasha whispers way too loudly.

"Shut up!" I snap. "Fucking focus. You have one fucking job. Get Ashley to 10AK nightclub at 10:30 p.m. sober!"

"Yes, sir." Natasha giggles as she links arms with Jenna.

"Take her out for dinner and order water to drink. No more alcohol whatsoever," I demand.

"Yes," Jenna replies. "Good idea." She kisses my cheek. "I'm on the job, Cameron. Don't worry. I've got this."

Hmm. Jenna seems less drunk than the other two.

Natasha scrunches up her face and puts her hand on her hip. "Well, how the fuck are we supposed to say no more drinks to Ashley?"

"I don't know. Figure it out!" I growl in a whisper.

I walk back around the corner to see Ashley laughing with Joshua. He glances up and smirks at me with a mischievous look in his eye. He knows this is a royal fuck up and he thinks it's hilarious.

"We ready to go?" I ask. "I think the girls are going out for dinner now."

"Yes," Natasha blurts. "I'm starving."

"Oh, me, too," Jenna agrees.

Ashley screws up her face. "Really? I'm not hungry at all. Eating's cheating. Nobody eats in Vegas."

Joshua and Adrian burst out laughing and I inhale deeply.

This night will be the fucking death of me.


## 10AK NIGHTCLUB - 11pm

I watch the man talking to Ashley with my heart slamming against my chest.

This is it.

Everyone is over in the corner and the security guards are along the wall.

I grip the ring with white-knuckle force in my pocket.

*Fuck.*

I've never been so nervous.

I see Ashley start to look around for her friends.

Go-time.

Holy fucking fuck!

I make my way over to them. "Is there a problem here?" I ask.

"Who are you?" the guy sneers.

"None of your business," I reply.

Ashley starts to look around for our security guards.

"Is this dead shit your husband?" the guy asks.

Ashley is looking around for the others as she gets nervous. "No this is."

My heart hammers hard as I watch her, and I drop to my knee and pull out the ring.

She turns back to me and her eyes widen.

"I'd like to be your husband for real." I grin up at her, full of hope. "This time in Vegas, things will be different."

Tears fill her eyes and an unfamiliar emotion runs through me as I smile softly.

I wish I could bottle this moment.

She looks over to our friends, who are all bouncing on the spot.

"I should have trusted my gut instincts and taken you straight to the chapel and married you that night," I whisper.

She puts her hands over her mouth in shock.

"Will you marry me, Ashley Tucker?"

She laughs and bends to kiss me. The crowd cheers around us.

Our faces are scrunched together, and she clings onto me with excitement. I stand and slowly slide the ring onto her finger. She holds her hand out to look at it and then looks back up at me.

"You didn't answer me," I whisper as I wrap her in my arms. "Say it out loud."

"Yes, I'll marry you." She laughs. "You are the best fake husband I could have ever asked for."

Our lips meet as she wraps her arms around me and I know, without a doubt, that I am the luckiest man on Earth.

# CHAPTER 4

**Ashley**

THE MORNING SUN peeks through the blinds and I can hear the birds chirping outside our window. The room is semi-dark, and the sound of Cam's breathing as he sleeps is the only things to be heard. I hold out my hand and stare at the engagement ring on my finger, a broad smile crossing my face.

I can't believe it.

I actually cannot believe it.

I'm getting married, and not married to just anybody—I'm getting married to Cameron Stanton, the man of my dreams—the man of every woman's dreams.

How did I ever score this? I thought I was simply getting a slutty, hot hookup in Vegas and I somehow ended up pregnant... to someone who turned out to be the perfect male specimen.

*What were the chances?*

How in the heck has everything that was once so wrong turned out to be so right?

It's been a week today since Cam asked me to marry him with the perfect Vegas proposal, in the same place, at the same time, in the same scenario as we first met. I have floated through seven blissful days, and even though Cam and I are always tight, and things are normally pretty great between us, I feel like this week has been a turning point.

We can't get enough of each other.

Literally.

We kiss in the car like school kids. I don't want to go anywhere without him and he has been looking at me like I'm the only woman in the world. It's as if a new, deeper level of intimacy has been reached between us. He was so proud this week to tell everyone that we are getting married. I can't wait to be his wife.

*We're getting married!*

It feels like now we know that this really is forever, everything has changed and somehow become deeper.

I bring my hand closer to my face, study my ring, and I smile. It's the most beautiful thing I have ever seen. Exactly what I would have picked, even if it is a bit big. Cameron was concerned it wasn't big enough.

Typical Cameron.

"Will you stop looking at that ring?" Cameron whispers huskily.

I turn and softly kiss him on the lips. "I can't." I turn back and study it again. "I still can't believe you asked me to marry you."

"Hmm," he hums sleepily with his eyes closed. "How else am I ever going to get you to grant me anal sex?"

My mouth falls open in shock and I burst out laughing.

"Every single time your romance score rises, you open your stupid big mouth and crash-tackle it back to zero."

He smiles with his eyes still closed. "Well..." He brings his hand up to behind his head. "You did say that you were saving your ass for your husband."

I giggle and kiss his big, stupid lips.

He raises his eyebrow. "And I am a goal-orientated man, you know."

I laugh. "I think you told me about your goals on the first night you met me." I smile and look back at my ring. "When you wanted to consummate our fake marriage."

He rolls over quickly so that he's on top of me. "That's when you told me you were saving yourself for your husband." His dark eyes drop to my lips.

"You're not my husband yet," I whisper.

He bends and catches my bottom lip between his teeth, pulling it to him. "I'm going to be your husband very soon." He reaches down and circles his fingers over my clitoris, and then as his eyes hold mine he slides two fingers deep into my sex. My back arches off the bed in approval.

I watch him watching me.

He slowly pulses his thick fingers in and out as he watches my face in wonder. His lips move to my ear and he bites down hard. I wince at the feel of his teeth on my skin.

"When I'm your wife you can do whatever you want with me," I breathe.

His eyes flicker with arousal. "I intend to," he whispers. "And you're going to love every fucking hard inch of it." He pushes three fingers in aggressively, and I moan in pleasure. He starts to work me hard, then harder, and the bed is rocking as I ride his thick, strong fingers.

"Do you like that, Bloss?" he whispers as he watches my face. "My dirty little fiancée."

I smile and close my eyes. God, he's so good at this.

*G spot... every damn time.*

He strokes it, pumps it and stretches me wide, causing my mouth to drop open from the pleasure. "Oh..." I moan, my legs opening farther without instruction. I need him deeper. "God," I whimper. He's been touching me for all of two minutes and I already can't take a second more.

I need him now.

He slides beneath the blankets and my eyes fall to the open door. "Cam, the door," I breathe.

He goes lower and lower, and he nips my hipbones with his teeth. I jump off the bed and bring my hands to the back of his head. He throws my legs over his broad shoulders and drops his lips to my sex. I hear him inhale deeply and my eyes roll back in my head. Fuck, he's so damn hot. Then he really starts to go to town. Long, deep licks tease me, followed by a slow suck and then a nibble of my clitoris... the perfect trifecta.

Again and again.

Cameron Stanton is the king of oral.

There isn't a woman on Earth who wouldn't orgasm within one-minute-flat with this technique, and I'm no different.

My breath begins to quiver as my body loses control, and my fingers instinctively run through his hair.

He adds his fingers in time with his tongue and that's it.

I can't hold it.

I bring my legs up as I try to deal with the sensory overload. "Open your fucking legs!" he growls as he slams them back against the mattress.

One more deep lick, and my whole body convulses forward

as an orgasm rips through me. Before I can react, he has my legs lifted over his shoulders and he slams into me.

"Fuck, yeah," he whispers in my ear.

He kisses me, and I can taste my own salty arousal on his lips, feel it in his stubble and, holy fuck, this man is off the charts.

Then he's riding me hard. Deep, punishing hits. All I can do is cling to him as his body takes what it needs from mine. Perspiration dusts his skin and his hair falls over his forehead as he concentrates.

He widens his knees to give himself better control and really lets me have it.

Ah, shit, the door. I glance over at it again. "The door, Cam," I whisper.

"Shut up and fuck me," he growls. He turns his head to kiss my ankle and the sight of him tenderly caressing my foot as his cock near rips me in half is a sensory overload. I close my eyes to try and hold it off.

"Look at me," he whispers as he grabs my jaw and drags my face to his. "Do you feel that, Ash?" He pumps me hard. "This is the only cock you're going to feel ever again." He kisses my ankle softly once more.

Oh, God...

I can't hold it. I lurch forward as my orgasm rips through me, and he holds deep as his body empties itself into mine.

He falls onto me and I stare at the ceiling. We're both covered in perspiration and breathing heavily. "I can't wait to fuck your ass that hard." He smiles sarcastically against my shoulder.

My eyes widen. "For the record, Cameron Stanton, you are never fucking my ass that hard," I mutter dryly.

He lifts himself up onto his elbow and looks down at me.

"My wife. My ass. My way." He raises his eyebrow in a silent challenge.

I widen my eyes and shake my head. "You do know that your romantic score is now sitting at negative two, right?"

He kisses me on the lips, tenderly. "I don't need a romantic score because I know I can give you a ten right here." He flexes his dick inside of me. "I also know that you are a sex maniac." He winks cheekily. "So, that works in my favor."

"You're off the scale between the sheets." I smirk, because he really is ridiculously good in bed. "It's immeasurable, actually."

He slowly pulls out of me as he laughs that beautiful carefree laugh before he falls beside me on the mattress. He slides his arm under my head and pulls my body half over his. "Well, then... Seeing that my life's goal has always been to have an immeasurable cock..." He kisses my forehead. "My work here is done."

"Negative five," I reply flatly.

He laughs out loud and I feel it all the way to my bones. "Shut up or I'll fuck you again, Tucker."

———

"How much farther?" Owen whines from the back seat.

"Not long, buddy," Cam replies as he glances at the Google Maps on the dashboard. We seem to have been travelling through the countryside for a long, long time, pastures new for as far as our eyes can see.

It's Saturday and we're on our way to San Diego to see the property I inherited from Gloria. Well, the property *we* inherited.

We haven't had time to look at the other house in town yet, but for some reason this is the one I'm dying to see the most.

"So, tomorrow?" Cam says.

"Yes?" I reply.

"I thought we might go and look at a few wedding reception venues."

"We have heaps of time to do that."

His eyes flicker to me. "Well, not really. We're going to have trouble getting in somewhere as it is."

I look over at him. "What? They don't have one booking available next year?" I roll my eyes. Him and this damn organization fetish.

"What are you talking about? Next year? I want to get married next month."

I scrunch up my face. "What? That's ridiculous."

"When were you thinking?" He frowns.

"Not next month, for God's sake," I mutter. "I want to lose at least five kilos before I get married. I haven't got a dress or anything."

He shakes his head in disgust. "You are not losing any weight. Wake up to yourself, woman. You're perfect just the way you are."

That's a bit cute. I smile at him and he reaches over to take my hand in his, placing it on his lap as he thinks.

"I need at least twelve months, Cam."

"No."

"What do you mean *no*?" I ask.

"I want to be married now. Why on Earth would you need twelve months?"

"I need to get a dress, find a venue, organize everything." I shake my head. "This is overwhelming, and you know how time-poor I am already."

He thinks for a moment. "Well." He shrugs. "I'll organize it.

You just need to pick the venue and your dress. I'll do everything else."

*He'll do everything else? As if!*

I know for a fact that he has already lined Adrian up for the job. Adrian rang me on the Monday morning we got back from Vegas to discuss color palettes. "Don't you mean Adrian will do everything else?" I ask.

He shrugs. "You know Murph loves weddings and shit."

"Don't say shit, Dad," Owen calls from the backseat.

"Sorry," he replies with a roll of his eyes. "Fucking *shit*," he mouths so Owen can't hear.

I smirk. Watching him getting his language picked up by his goody two-shoes son really is amusing.

We drive for a moment and I can see his brain ticking at a million miles a minute. "Just pick the venue and Adrian and I will organize everything." His eyes find mine. "All you have to do is buy a dress and show up on the day. I know how busy you are."

"What's the rush?" I ask.

His eyes continually flicker between the road and me. "Well, I've done it now. As far as I'm concerned we're already married."

*Already married.*

I smile broadly. Well, if that isn't the most perfect piece of information I have ever heard.

"We're not married, Cam." I smile.

His hand slides up my thigh and under my dress. "It can't come soon enough for me, Bloss."

"You do know I love you, right?" I smile broadly.

He smiles sarcastically as he looks at his son in the rearview mirror. "Yes. Everyone in the car loves me. I'm a rock star."

"Oh, man." Owen sighs. "He's doing that great thing again, Mom."

I laugh. "Yes, he is Owen."

*"Destination is on your left,"* our map lady tells us, and Cameron brings the car down to a slow roll.

"Is this it?" Cam frowns as he looks up the long driveway.

I shuffle through the papers and retrieve the address to read it out.

"Yes, this is it." He frowns as he looks around.

A long pebble driveway that disappears into the paddocks is in front of us, and it has an old letterbox with a little plaque hanging down.

### Pemberley

"What's Pemberley?" Cameron frowns.

I scramble through the papers. "I don't know." I read the paperwork again. "Oh, look, it's the name of the property." I bunch my shoulders up excitedly and Cam raises his eyebrows in surprise.

My mouth falls open in surprise. "Oh, Cam. That's the name of Mr. Darcy's property."

"Pretty cool," he mutters under his breath. We turn in to the driveway and start up the long pebble driveway that disappears up into the distance. There're green fields for as far as we can see with huge oak trees sporadically planted throughout the property.

"This is beautiful." I smile in wonder as I look around at the lush, green countryside.

"Oh look, Mom," Owen calls excitedly. "Look at that huge climbing tree."

I laugh as we keep going. "This is a super-long driveway."

"Sure is!" he yells.

We keep going and going and going, and I feel like a little

kid on Christmas morning. I grab Cameron's hand and hold it in mine. "This is so exciting, Cam."

He smiles and kisses the back of my hand. He's loving this. Owen and I are literally bouncing in our seats.

Finally, a house comes into view, but it's hard to make out from a distance. "Is that the house?" I crane my neck as I try to see.

"I think so," Cam mutters as he concentrates.

"I can't see it. I can't see it," Owen calls from the backseat.

"We'll be there soon, buddy and you can see it then," Cam replies.

As it gets closer, coming more into focus, the car falls silent. It's white with a green tin roof, two stories with a big wrap-around veranda. It looks like it would have been a stately home back in its day. I say back in its day because in the present time it looks absolutely dilapidated.

Cam pulls the car to a stop and we all sit and stare at it for a moment.

Wow.

Cam's eyes flicker over to me as if scared to say anything. I swallow the lump in my throat and slowly open the car door.

I take the keys and Owen climbs out of the car, bouncing toward the tree.

"Owen. Stay with me, please," Cam calls.

The veranda has wide floorboards that have worn through in some places. The posts have no paint left on them, and you can't see through the windows because they're so dirty.

"Is this safe to go in?" Cam frowns.

I shrug. "She did say that nobody has been here for ten years," I reply as I peer in through the window. I shrug. "Come on." I grab the keys and try to open the door, but the key doesn't fit. I try another and another, having no luck.

"Here, give them to me. "Cam takes the keys and shuffles through them as he tries to unlock the door. I pick up Owen and put him on my hip. We turn back to look out over the property and my breath catches. It has the most beautiful view I have ever seen, with green rolling hills and mountains in the distance. There're so many beautiful oak trees and a tranquility that I don't think I've ever felt. "Gosh, it's so beautiful here," I whisper.

"Glad you think so," Cam mutters as he bangs the door. It opens with a loud creak. The three of us peer in like scared children.

Cameron's eyes widen in horror and I break into a stupid smile. The foyer is grand and leads onto a huge family room, and the stairs are up in front. It's bad... like really bad. The floorboards are all caving in and the walls are all bowed. In the middle of the family room, it looks as though a part of the ceiling has fallen and crashed onto the floor. Luckily, there's no furniture. It's empty apart from the plasterboard everywhere.

Cameron takes Owen from me immediately. "I don't think this is safe to go farther into," he whispers.

I walk in and around through the family room. There's a formal dining room and another room—I'm not sure what this is. The kitchen is at the back and I smile broadly. It's bright green and horrible. I imagine Gloria back in her day cooking in here. Another three rooms are over to the left behind the staircase, although I have no idea what they would have been used for.

"It's big." I frown.

Cameron follows me in silence with Owen on his hip.

"This is sick," Owen calls.

"Yes, Owen, this is sick," Cameron mutters dryly. "This is

one of those vomit-inducing, sick places. It smells old and musty."

I walk over to the stairs. "I wonder what's upstairs..."

"Ashley, I don't think the stairs are safe," Cameron calls. "Look, one is missing."

The second step is missing the timber and I jump over it, taking them two at a time until I find a grand hallway, six bedrooms, and a broken-down bathroom. The roof obviously has a leak because there are brown stains that have marked the walls in the hall. The carpet is threadbare, and you can see the floorboards through it.

I walk into the master bedroom and look through the window out onto the beautiful meadows below, where I see a large, blue-stone barn out the back. "Cameron come up here. You have got to see this," I call excitedly.

"I don't think I want to," he calls.

I hear him and Owen slowly make their way up the stairs, looking through the house before they come and find me in the master suite.

I smile as I stare out the window. "Look..." I point excitedly.

Cameron peers down at the barn and tries to force a smile. "The land is nice," he murmurs. He looks around. "I think a bulldozer is the best thing for the house, though."

I smile. "Are you kidding me? No way," I whisper.

He frowns.

"We have to fix this house up. Bring it back to its former glory like Gloria and her husband had it." I smile, filled with hope.

He shakes his head. "Ash, no building company would take this on. The job is too big."

I peer through the window and grin. "No, Cam, we're going to do everything ourselves."

He looks at me blankly.

"Can you imagine the fun we would have? I want us to do this house up ourselves. Just me, you, and Owen."

"That's ridiculous." He looks around in disgust. "I know nothing about anything like that."

I smile and wrap my arms around him and Owen. "Oh, this is just perfect."

He scowls as he looks around. "Ashley..." He stops himself as his eyes roam the room. "I'm sorry to say, but this house is appalling."

"No. It's the opposite, Cam; it's so beautiful." I smile as I hold my arms out wide. "Can you imagine how amazing we could make this house?"

He turns up his nose. "You have a perfect house in L.A. to call your own."

"I don't want a perfect house, Cam. I want one that I have to work for. One that I can bring back to life myself."

Cameron's eyes widen in horror. "No amount of renovating can fix this, Ash. I'm sorry. I know you were excited."

I throw my hands in the air. "I'm thrilled."

"With this?" He shakes his head. "Ash..." He puts Owen down and walks over to the door. When he pushes it back it falls from its hinges and drops with a loud crash, and he jumps back out of the way. "This place is so damn dangerous," he cries.

Owen and I burst out laughing.

"You are such a snob." I smile as I stare back out the window. "Come on, let's go look at the barn." I take off downstairs with them following me, and we walk out the back. About two-hundred meters from the house and across a green lush paddock sits the large, blue-stone barn. It's locked with a big rusty padlock. "Where are the keys?" I ask.

Cameron frowns and digs them out of his pocket. He slowly begins to try all the keys, and when the last one works he slowly opens the doors.

The roof is open with big, dark, timber rafters, while the floor is stone. "Oh, this is amazing," I gasp.

Cameron looks around the barn, deadpan. "This place is woeful."

I laugh. "Oh, let's go back to town, buy some camping supplies, and stay here tonight." I smile hopefully.

"Yes!" Owen squeals.

"Let's not," Cameron mutters. "You couldn't pay me enough to stay out here. God knows what could happen." He kicks a rock that's in front of his feet as he looks around. "This is not a fucking episode of the Amityville Horror House, you know."

I laugh and put my hand over my mouth as I look around. He really is freaking out here.

"Dad..." Owen corrects him.

"Owen!" Cameron snaps as he loses his last inch of patience. "I am a grown man and I can swear when I want to. You are the only one not allowed to swear around here. Stop correcting me."

Owen widens his eyes at me. "Jeez," he whispers under his breath.

"Can we stay the night, Cam?" I smile hopefully.

"Absolutely not," he replies as he leaves the barn and starts to walk back to the house.

"Why not?" I call.

He turns to face me and counts on his fingers. "Where do I start, Ashley? There's no power, no running water, no bathroom. Things are falling off the hinges. This place is a death trap!"

I smile and shrug. "So?"

His eyes widen. "This is horrible. I can't stay here, and I won't have you two stay here, either." He turns to walk back to the front. "This is worse than third-world."

"Well, I'm coming back here next weekend," I call.

"Great," he shouts back as he opens the door to our car. "You do that while Owen and I arrange our wedding in L.A." He rolls his eyes. "It's not like we have nothing to do back home or anything." He shakes his head in disgust.

"Okay." I smile as I call after him. I look around the house once more before I lock it up and climb into the car.

Cameron looks at me blankly.

I smile at the big old house. "See you next weekend, Pemberley," I call.

"Bye," Owen cries.

"Good riddance," Cameron mutters as he starts the car. "Let's go find some coffee."

# CHAPTER 5

**Ashley**

"AND OUT HERE IS WHERE we serve cocktails at dusk," the snooty wedding planner says with her plum-in-mouth accent.

"Ah, yes, lovely." Cameron smiles enthusiastically as he looks around.

I walk behind them both like a petulant child. The gardens are perfect. The whole thing is perfect. But it's Sunday and we're now at the sixth wedding reception venue of the day.

They're snobby, snooty, pretentious, and wanky... even if they're all perfectly beautiful.

Cameron turns and holds his hand out to me, and I take it in mine. "This one is nice, Bloss." He smiles hopefully.

"Yeah." I sigh, unimpressed as I look around.

"What's wrong with this one?" Cameron whispers, sensing my disapproval.

I shrug and look around. "Nothing, it's fine."

"Fine?" Cam repeats as he rolls his eyes. "This is not fine. This is amazing."

I sigh. "If you say so."

"And out here is where the dancing in the marquee will take place after the formal dinner." She points to the trees. "The trees come alive at night with the fairy lights. It's so romantic and a real sight to behold," she purrs as she keeps walking up a fancy garden path to show us something else.

I scowl. "A real sight to behold?" I mouth behind her back.

Cameron smirks and slaps my ass. "Stop it. Will you behave yourself?" he whispers.

We come to a circular private clearing with a bar, table, and chairs sitting in the center of it. "And over here we have the cigar bar." She smiles.

Cameron's eyes light up. "Cigar bar? Oh, I like that."

"We have over two-hundred different types of cigars that your guests may pick from, as well as specialty spirits which will be exclusive to your honored guests."

I roll my eyes. I've never heard anything more ridiculous.

She turns to show us something else down another path.

"Can we go?" I whisper.

"No," Cameron whispers back. "I like this place."

"I'm not getting married here."

"Why not?"

"I hate it."

"Fucking pick somewhere then, Ashley," he whispers with a fake smile plastered on his face. "There's been nothing wrong with any of the places I've taken you today. If this place doesn't excite you, I have no idea where will."

"I would rather be married in a registry office than in any of these wanky places you've brought me to."

He takes my hand and smiles as the lady turns to see what's taking us so long. She turns back to the front.

"Well..." Cameron whispers. "Owen and I want a nice wedding day. That doesn't involve a registry office."

I roll my eyes and exhale loudly. "You just pick somewhere then."

He frowns. "Why are you being difficult?"

"Why are you being a snob?"

His face falls. "Where do you want to get married? Fucking McDonald's?"

"It's better than this crap!" I snap. "I know Owen would definitely like McDonald's better, too."

Cameron rolls his eyes and walks forward to listen to the next lot of drivel about how exquisite this place is.

I keep trudging behind them, hating every word that comes out of her mouth.

Who knew picking a wedding venue would be so painful?

———

It's Tuesday afternoon. I'm just leaving work, walking through the parking lot toward my car, when my phone rings.

"Hello, Ashley, this is Marissa," the kind voice says through an obvious smile.

"Hi, Marissa." I smile. Marissa is one of Cameron's PAs. She goes into surgery with him.

"Dr. Stanton has just asked me to call you to let you know that his back is playing up and he has a massage therapist coming to the house tonight at eight, so he'll be having the massage in his office."

I frown. "Oh."

"He just wanted me to call ahead in case the therapist gets

there a few minutes before he does." Cameron gets a really tight back from being hunched over in surgery for so long, but he usually goes to the massage therapy place on a Friday afternoon. It must be really acting up.

"Yes, that's fine, thanks for the warning." I laugh. "Actually, that's a great idea. Can you ask Cameron if he can book me in one, too, after him, please?" I ask. My back has been as tight as all hell this week, too.

"Yes, of course. Goodbye."

I make it to the car and start my journey home when my phone rings again through the Bluetooth. "Hello," I answer.

"Hi, it's me again," Marissa says.

"Hi, Marissa." I smile.

"Umm..." She pauses. "Dr. Stanton asked me to call you back to say that the massage therapist wouldn't be able to do that tonight, but he'll book you something for tomorrow."

"Oh, okay, no worries," I reply. "Thank you." I turn the corner and end the call. Oh, well. Damn it. I could have done with a massage tonight.

———

At 7:50 p.m. the doorbell rings. Cameron isn't home from surgery yet but his massage therapist has arrived.

I answer the door and my eyes widen. Suddenly I'm self-conscious because of my daggy attire.

"Hello." The tall, muscular blond smiles. "I'm Steven. I'm here for Cameron."

He's huge and he's wearing all white clothing with a massage table tucked under his arm. He smells like massage oil.

Holy hell. He's just so...

"What?" Oh. I shake my head in embarrassment. "Please...

come in." I gesture to the hall. "I think he said you were to set up in the office."

He smiles, as if knowing my wayward thoughts. He has a dimple in his chin and I find myself smiling goofily as I follow him up the hall.

Wow, this guy is off the charts hot.

"Just in here?" he asks sexily.

Huh... Well, will you look at that? God damn bona fide hot masseuse. Who knew they even existed?

"Yes." I smile, remembering where I am.

I hear the gates open and I know my man is home. "Cameron won't be a minute." I smile as I leave the room. "Nice to meet you, Steven," I call.

Cameron comes in the front door and kisses me quickly on the lips. "Sorry, Bloss. Is he here?"

"Yes, in your office."

He walks down to the laundry, takes his scrubs off, and throws them in the washing machine. "I need a quick shower." He looks around. "Where's Owen?"

"Oh, he went to bed early. He fell asleep on the couch."

Cameron's face falls with disappointment and he walks up to his office in his briefs. "Just a quick shower, man. I won't be five minutes."

"Okay," I hear Steven reply.

Cam closes the door as he leaves the office and goes bouncing up the stairs.

I walk out and flick on the kettle. Hmm, it really is a pity I'm not getting a massage tonight.

I frown as I make my tea. Hang on a minute...

I bet Cameron didn't even ask if I could have a massage tonight. He doesn't want me to get a massage because Steven is off the fucking charts hot.

I smirk. Interesting.

————

An hour and a half later, a very sleepy and relaxed Cameron walks Steven to the front door. "Thank you." He smiles.

He then comes to me on the couch and I stand and put my arms around his neck. "Hey, babe." He smiles softly as he takes me in his arms.

"Have you eaten?" I kiss his lips.

"Hmm, yeah. I had some sushi in the car on the way home." He sighs as he puts his head down onto my shoulder. He really is exhausted.

"How come I couldn't get a massage tonight?" I ask.

"You can get a massage," he replies as he feels my behind. "Just not by him."

I smile. "Why not?"

Cameron frowns. "I don't want his hands on you."

"Why? Because he's good-looking?"

"He's not touching you. End of discussion." He pulls out of my grip and turns toward the stairs.

"Well, that's ridiculous," I call after him.

"I know what these guys are like. A hot chick like you? His hands would be everywhere."

My mouth falls open.

"He's not fucking touching my girl."

"How come you go to him, then?"

"Because he's the best."

I put my hands on my hips. "Cameron, are you serious?"

"Deadly."

I shake my head and lock up, then I turn the lights off and go upstairs to find Cam already in bed. I tear the quilt back in a huff. "That's the most ridiculous thing I've ever heard."

"Bullshit. Ask Natasha about her hot massage therapist back in Sydney."

"What about him?" I snap as I get into bed.

"He bones chicks. Gives them a happy ending at the end of their massage."

"He does not."

"Does too. A whole parlor of them who fuck chicks who get massages."

"Oh... like every other massage parlor for men, you mean?" I reply sarcastically as I roll my back to him. "You're making this shit up. How would you know this, anyway?

"Natasha got drunk and told Josh that she had a massage with a happy ending."

My eyes widen, and I get the giggles as I imagine Joshua going crazy ballistic. I'm going to have to ask her about this.

"Well, I just have a tight back. I want a massage with a relaxed ending," I tell him.

"He's not touching you, Ashley. Ever. Move on."

I smirk in the darkness. He's fun to tease. "Well, if I can't have Steven as a massage therapist, you can't have female PAs."

"Oh, God." He sighs. "And what's that supposed to mean?"

"Well..." I smirk. "You could run off with a PA and fuck her in the storeroom, how would I know?"

"I specifically don't hire PAs that I'm attracted to. I'm not an idiot, Ashley. You don't get your meat where you get your potatoes."

My mouth falls open in shock and I roll onto my back. "Did you just tell me that you don't get your meat where you get you potatoes? Meaning work is potatoes? And meat is vaginas?"

"I did. Now go to sleep." He exhales as he starts to relax.

"And if you dare think of Steven again I will crack your back myself."

I smile into the darkness.

"Don't smile, it's going to hurt." He exhales again. "A lot."

———

I drop another load of stuff outside the front door. "Okay, so I have the chairs, the sleeping bags, the air mattresses, the pump, food. What else do we need, Owen?" I think out loud.

Owen shrugs with a broad smile.

"Oh, cleaning stuff." I go and retrieve the broom, mop, and cleaning cloths, as well as the bucket and sprays from the store-room. Cameron is lying on the couch reading the paper as I walk past him with everything.

"Are you sure you're not coming, Cameron?" I ask.

It's Saturday morning and Owen and I are getting ready for our night at Pemberley. Cameron is being a stick in the mud and doesn't want anything to do with it.

"Nope." He calls over his paper. "I'm relaxing. Pemberley isn't for me." He flicks the page in annoyance. "It is the week-end, you know."

I smirk. "The power and water are now on at Pemberley, so that's good."

"Hmm."

"Will it be scary there without Dad, Mom?" Owen asks as his little eyes flicker between us.

I shrug. "Nope, we can do this, buddy. We're tough. We'll see Dad late tomorrow night when we get back."

Cameron glares at me over the top of his paper, and I turn my back to him and smirk.

I'm giving him the reverse psychology treatment all the way

to Pemberley. "It will be nice for Daddy to have a night here to himself," I say to Owen.

Big pussy. He hates being here alone.

Owen walks over to his father and takes his hand. "Can't you come, Dad?"

"No, buddy." Cameron sighs, clearly feeling guilty.

I smirk as I keep getting the things ready. "Owen, go and grab your sweater. We'll have a campfire tonight. I bought marshmallows to roast on sticks."

"Yes!" Owen cries in excitement. "Where will we get the wood?"

"I don't know yet. We'll find some." Owen runs upstairs excitedly.

"Burn the house," Cameron replies flatly.

I smile as I start to take everything outside to load it into the car. It takes me three trips to get everything in. "Okay, that's it. Let's go, Owen."

"Yes." Owen runs outside.

"Coming out to say goodbye, babe?" I ask Cameron as I walk out the front door.

He throws his paper down, drags himself off the couch, and walks out to the car.

"I can't believe you're actually going without me," he murmurs.

"I can't believe that you don't want to come," I reply as I throw Owen his little leather working gloves as he sits in the backseat.

"What are these?" he asks excitedly.

"Your working gloves. I got you some working boots, too, big boy."

His eyes widen in excitement. "Awesome."

Cameron frowns. "I don't want him working on that house."

I roll my eyes. "That's exactly why we're going, Cameron, so he can learn that just because his daddy has money doesn't mean he gets things for free."

Cameron looks at me, deadpan.

"I want him to be proud of what we build and renovate." I smile softly up at Cam and he frowns. "This is like the ultimate family hobby. Something that we can achieve together."

Cameron rolls his eyes in an over-dramatic fashion.

"And you're in this family, Cameron." I widen my eyes to accentuate my point.

He shakes his head. "Do you have any shovels packed?"

"What for?" I ask.

"Grave digging!" he snaps. "Give me ten minutes."

"Your things are already in the car." I smile broadly.

He looks at me, deadpan. "Did you just play me?"

"Like a fiddle." I kiss him softly on the lips and he shakes his head.

"You're a pain in my ass, Tucker."

"But you love me, right?"

"Unfortunately." He marches inside and ten minutes later he reappears, all showered and ready with a case of wine under his arm. "I need alcohol if I'm staying in that hell hole."

"Already packed and in the car." I tap my temple. "Up here for thinking..."

He raises an eyebrow and points to my sex. "And down there for dancing?" He slams Owen's car door shut. "My only goal this weekend is to pop that airbed with your body." He gets in and starts the car. "Get in, Tucker, before Owen and I leave you here."

. . .

"Mom, it's nearly time to get it started. Come look," Owen calls in excitement.

I walk out of the barn to see my men's afternoon handiwork, and I smile broadly. It's dusk, and we've been working all day. I've swept and cleaned the barn. We decided to sleep out here tonight. It's in much better condition than the house is, and we know that if it rains the roof definitely doesn't leak. The stone wall and floor are both rock-solid. I've prepared our beds and sleeping bags, and I'm just finishing with the windows. "Wow." I raise my eyebrows. "Impressive."

Owen and Cameron built a fire pit together. They cleared a space, collected rocks, and then placed them carefully in a circle, four high. They have three folding chairs positioned around it, and the marshmallows are front and center with three long toasting sticks ready.

I throw down my window-cleaning rags and take a seat by the fire.

Cameron's face falls as he thinks. "Do we have any matches?"

I raise my eyebrows. "Didn't you think of that before you started building this?" I ask.

"No." Cameron sighs as he drags his hand down his face.

Owen's little shoulders slump in disappointment.

"Lucky I was a Girl Scout," I tease. I go to my supplies bag and pull out a cigarette lighter I brought from home. I've thought of everything... I hope. I pass the lighter to Cameron and he lights the paper they have scrunched up around the kindling, and it slowly starts to take off.

"Mom, quick take a photo of me and Dad with our fire to send to Jenna," Owen says, wide-eyed.

Cameron smiles a proud of himself smile.

I dig out my phone. "Great idea, Owie."

76

Cameron puts his arm around Owen's shoulders and they pose as I click away.

Owen then sits on his little fold-up chair and watches the fire, his legs swinging with glee as he smiles from ear to ear.

Cam watches him silently and I can see him thinking. His eyes flicker to me, and he smiles softly.

I think he just had an 'aha' moment as he watches how proud his son is of making a fire. He comes and takes a seat next to me on his camp chair, puts his hand on my thigh, and kisses my lips. "I do love you."

I smile against him. "What's not to love?"

"Give me your phone, Mom." Owen demands. "Let me take a photo of you two."

Cam and I smile as Owen snaps away.

We toast marshmallows and play I Spy, and we make toast with jam, too. I don't think I've ever had a nicer night. Cam and I have drunk a bottle of red and I'm sitting with my legs draped over his while he and Owen play rock, paper, scissors. To be honest, this is the most relaxed that I've been in such a very long time. No internet, no television, no distractions. The only sound that can be heard is the sporadic crackling of the fire. I look across the paddock and up at the old house, and I wonder if Gloria is up in Heaven watching us.

I bet she's smiling.

She told me I would find my Mr. Darcy and I did. I'm marrying him and he's here on the very same farm, maybe at the very same place, where she sat with her Mr. Darcy.

I look back over to watch my two boys laugh freely, and I become emotional, tearing up.

For the first time in so long I feel as if everything has clicked into place.

My son, my job, my future husband, and this house... I feel

like it was all meant to be, and maybe it's the red wine talking, but at this moment I could happily live here on this farm without one cent to my name.

I have everything that I could ever want right here.

The fire's dying down. It's late. We've been sitting around it for hours. "Come on. Bedtime, mister," Cam tells Owen.

We stand and make our way into the barn to change into our pajamas, and I close the door. Owen dives onto his airbed and Cameron stands at the end of the bed with his hands on his hips as he studies our surroundings. "Is this even fucking safe?" he whispers under his breath.

"Oh, yeah," Owen calls out excitedly. "This bed is sick!"

I giggle as I climb onto the airbed and get into my sleeping bag while Cameron walks the perimeter of the barn with the light on his phone turned on.

"What are you doing?" I call.

"Looking for rats. I don't particularly want my ear chewed off in the middle of the night. They're most welcome to yours, though. You could do with some otoplasty."

I laugh and lie back onto the bed. I glance over, and Owen is already sound asleep. He's worn out from carrying all those rocks today. After ten minutes of investigating, Cameron slides into his sleeping bag next to me and sits up to shine his light around once more.

"Will you relax?" I sigh sleepily.

"Fucking Amityville Horror. Here we go," he murmurs. "Who fucking knows what lives in this barn?"

"We do now," I whisper.

He exhales deeply. "You're lucky I love you, Bloss." He lies down. "I wouldn't do this shit for anyone else."

I smile broadly with my eyes closed. "I know."

––––––

"So, I was thinking that we just start by taking everything outside," I announce.

Cameron frowns as he looks at me. His hands are on his hips, encased in his leather working gloves, and he has his new steel-toed boots on that I bought him in secret over the week.

Owen is playing with his trucks on the front veranda.

"What do you mean?" He frowns as he looks at all the plasterboard everywhere on the ground. "What... all this?' He gestures to the pile of rubble.

"Yes." I pick up a piece and carry it outside to put it out on the grass to the side of the house.

I walk back inside to see Cameron's confused face. "What? You think that we're going to strip this house ourselves?"

"Uh-huh." I pick up another piece of plasterboard and disappear back outside before I come back in.

"Ashley, this job is too big for us. If you're that set on doing this hole up, we'll pay for someone to do it."

"No, we won't." I pick up another piece and take it outside. "We're doing everything ourselves, Cameron."

"It'll take years." He frowns.

I shrug. "So? We have years, don't we?" I pick up another piece and take it back outside, and I smile as I walk back in. He's secretly having a panic attack over there.

"Hang on, hang on." He puts his hands onto his hips. "So, you actually think that we can renovate this house ourselves?"

"Yes." I roll my eyes. "Are you listening to me at all?"

He shakes his head in disbelief. "How?"

I pick up another piece of plasterboard. "Not by standing

there watching, that's for sure." I take it outside and I smirk when I come back in.

"Well, I'm not sleeping in a damn barn, Ashley. I need a bathroom, at least," he demands.

"You can get the bathrooms done professionally," I concede as I pick up another piece of plasterboard. "We can sell the other house to pay for everything."

Cameron looks at me blankly, his hands still on his hips.

"You organize the bathrooms. Find a plumber and pick the tiles and fittings, and I'll clear the plasterboard." I pick up yet another piece.

"You're... You're fucking serious?" he stammers.

I nod.

He frowns. "Well, where will I find a plumber out here?"

I look at him, deadpan. "You're a heart surgeon, Cameron. I'm pretty sure you're smart enough to work this shit out." I carry out the next piece of plasterboard. "Oh, and I want a bathroom out in the barn, too, please!" I call.

"What for?"

"I'm making that a guesthouse so we can have friends stay over."

"Fuck's sake," I hear him mutter under his breath, and I bite my bottom lip to hide my smile. I come back inside.

"So that's four bathrooms I have to organize. How in the hell will I organize four bathrooms?"

It's really hard not to burst out laughing here. "I would start by writing a list and maybe Googling bathroom renovation."

He glares at me as I continue taking out my plasterboard.

"Well, it's going to have to wait until after the wedding."

"If you can't handle organizing a few tradesmen, just leave it." I sigh as I pick up more plasterboard. "I'll do it."

"I can handle it," he snaps.

"Doesn't look like you're handling it."

"And I thought the hard thing about marrying you was going to be proposing..." he mutters.

I turn to him. "No, Cam." I put my hands on my hips. "The hardest thing for you is going to be getting me pregnant and looking after our kids."

His eyes hold mine, and he smiles softly. "Now, there's a plan." He comes to me, brushes the hair back from my forehead, and kisses me softly.

"Renovating a house is easy, Cam." I look up at him. "It's going to be so rewarding to have done this ourselves. I know it's going to be hard, but can you imagine when we come here with the kids? The house will be finished, and we'll have a pool. They can have horses and motorbikes and know that we did all of this ourselves."

He looks around the house as he holds me in his arms.

"The whole thing is just overwhelming, Ash."

I smile. "You know what's overwhelming, Cam?"

"What?"

"Having a baby on your own. Not knowing who his father is. Don't talk to me about overwhelming because you have no fucking idea what it means."

He swallows the lump in his throat and blows out a breath. "You're a tough chick."

I smile broadly. "I am, so start moving this damn plasterboard before I hurt you." I smack his behind. "Now!"

———

It's 5:00 p.m. when I finally take one last look around Pemberley. Cameron and I have cleared the family room and half of the downstairs today. We're exhausted.

Owen has climbed trees and gotten into everything. The three of us are filthy dirty.

We walk down to the barn to get our things, and as Cameron loads himself up and disappears outside I stop and inhale my surroundings.

I love this stone barn. I love everything about it.

A thought crosses my mind and I go outside to look at the surrounding paddocks before I come back into the barn. It's big enough, sitting at about thirty meters long and about fifteen meters wide, but... no, it couldn't be possible.

Could it?

Cameron reappears through the doors.

"Cam." I bite my bottom lip nervously. How do I say this? "I think I know where I want to get married."

"Where, Bloss?" he mutters, distracted.

"Here. In this stone barn."

His face falls in horror. "You can't be serious."

# CHAPTER 6

**Ashley**

I SMILE, HOPEFUL. "COMPLETELY."

He shakes his head. "You're obviously having some kind of dust-induced delusional episode. Get in the car." He picks up the last of our bags. "Owen, get in the car, please," he calls. "Where is he?"

We walk outside to see Owen sliding down a tree trunk at full speed.

Cameron's eyes widen. "Be careful!" he calls in a fluster.

"Look, Cam." I grab his hand and lead him back inside. "Just listen to me for five minutes, please. Just five minutes."

He rolls his eyes.

I point to the back of the barn. "We could put a beautiful bathroom at the back for the guests." I point to the front. "We could put a carpeted clearing at the front where we could stand and get married. There could be a carpet down the center to create an aisle, or we could get married outside under the big oak tree." I run to the front of the barn as I try to pitch it to him. "We could rent beautiful seats, candles, lighting, and we could have musicians and fairy lights, too. Maybe circular tables with white chairs? We could employ caterers and hire a cocktail bar to put out on the lawn under the stars." I look around in excitement. "Lots of fresh flowers." I bounce up and down on the spot. "It could be so amazing."

He stares at me blankly.

"And the gardens... we could have a working bee out there with potted plants and a decorated entryway. It would probably cost the same as those swanky places you looked at." I shrug.

He looks around and exhales heavily. "Our guests won't want to come all the way out here, Ashley."

"The ones who matter will, and if they don't want to come then good riddance to them anyway."

I take his hand in mine. "Cam, I know you don't like this farm yet..." My eyes search his. "But you will. I promise, you will. And I want to get married somewhere that's sentimental to me, to us. Somewhere we're still going to love in fifty years' time."

"Marrying me isn't a big enough sentiment?"

I smile sadly. "Of course, it is." I look around and exhale. "You're right. It's okay if you don't want this." I shrug. "I understand." I smile and pick up the last of our bags. "It's got to be a joint decision, Cam. This is your wedding, too, and if you want to then we can just keep looking for a venue."

I walk out to the car and throw the bags into the trunk, then I strap Owen into his car seat. Cameron stays in the barn and I hold my breath. I know he's walking around, considering what I said.

*Please, please, please.*

He walks down the pebble driveway and looks around as I sit in the car, watching him.

"What's Dad doing?" Owen sighs. "Can we get McDonald's on the way home? I'm starving. I want nuggets."

I smile as I watch Cam doing his internal assessment. "Yes, baby. I'm getting a Big Mac," I reply.

Cameron finally gets into the car and slams the door, and his eyes flick over to me. "You're a pain in my ass, Tucker." He sighs.

"That's not a no." I smile hopefully.

He starts the car. "It isn't a yes, either."


## Cameron

I fasten the buttons on the white shirt I'm trying on. It's Wednesday afternoon and I'm in a menswear boutique looking at suits for the wedding with Joshua and Adrian. This was the only time the three of us could coordinate the same time off work in the next few weeks. Jenna is dropping off Owen soon.

"Well, what was so bad about it?" Adrian asks through the door.

"You should see this farm, Murph. You'll have a fucking conniption."

"It can't be that bad."

"Yep. This suit is good," Joshua calls out from his changing room.

"Leave it on. I want to see it," Murph tells him.

"It's worse than bad, it's…" I shake my head as I try to find a word bad enough, but there isn't one. "It's bulldozer material."

"And Ashley seriously wants you to do this up?" Adrian asks, surprised.

"Yes." I roll my eyes as I pull up the suit pants and zip them up. "Something about us working hard for something and it being a family project or some crap."

"Gray ties first, please," Adrian calls.

I shake my head and retrieve the gray tie from the chair. "She thinks it will be good for me and Owen," I reply.

The both stay silent as they dress.

"She says that just because Owen has a dad with money, she won't let him become spoiled, and she wants him to appreciate non-materialistic things... or something." I wrap the tie around my neck, frowning as I look at it. "How does this tie go again?" I ask.

"Ha," Adrian cries. "I love that girl, and it's a cravat. Hang on. I'll tie it."

"Yeah, well, if you love it so much then you get married in this bad version of Old McDonald Had a Farm!" I snap. "I get why she likes it, but seriously, this is going too far."

I hear Joshua chuckle in his changing room. "Blake loves that song," he snickers.

"Now she wants to get married in the barn..." I continue. "And I know how much she loves it so, obviously, I feel bad if I don't let her have it there." I shake my head in disgust. "I'm getting fucked up against the wall here..." I mutter. "Damned if I do and damned if I don't."

"What was the old lady's name? The one who left her this house?" Joshua asks.

"Gloria," I answer.

Joshua laughs. "So, effectively, Gloria left you a glory hole and you're the receiver."

Adrian chuckles. "Good one."

"Fuck off," I snap. "Although it's completely true." I pull my jacket on over my shoulders. "Ass-fucked. And there's another problem..." I add.

"What now?" Adrian asks.

"If we do have the wedding at the farm...where will we have our wedding night?" I shake my head at my predicament. "I want to take her someone nice for our first night together. I'm not spending my wedding night on a damn blow-up airbed in some barn."

They both laugh at my misfortune.

"Well..." Adrian thinks for a moment. "You could do up the master suite."

I frown as I process his suggestion.

"Oh my God. Yes. Do it up for her yourself in secret and surprise her with it on the wedding night as a gift."

I raise my eyebrows at the possibility.

"Huge brownie points. Fucking huge," Joshua says. "She would go ape if you did that for her."

"I wouldn't even know where to start, though," I reply.

"Happy wife, happy life, Cam..." Joshua murmurs.

Hmm. I guess that would be kind of cool to do for her. She *would* love it.

We all open the changing room doors at the same time and step out into the store to stand in a line in front of the mirror. Adrian smiles broadly, and Joshua slaps me on the back. "This is it, big boy."

Adrian secures our cravats and we all look at our reflections again. "Vests or no vests?" I ask.

"Vests," Adrian replies as he fusses with my tie. "But yours will be white," he adds.

I scrunch up my face. "I'm not a fan of a white vest, I'll feel like a pigeon. I think black."

"Black vest, black bowtie," Adrian replies.

"Okay, so where are the bowties?" I ask.

"Dad!" Owen calls as he runs into the store and jumps into my arms.

"Hey, buddy." I laugh as I catch him and kiss his perfect little head. "You ready to try on your suit?" I ask as I tickle his ribs.

"Uh-huh." Owen smiles goofily. He slaps hands with Joshua and Adrian in a greeting.

"Hey, big guy." Joshua rubs his hair affectionately.

Jenna's hands go to her mouth in excitement as she sees me. "You look gorgeous, Cam." She smiles.

"Hi, Jenna." I smirk as I lift the little black suit hung on a hanger from the back of my changing room door. "We going to try this on, Owen, so we can be ready for our wedding?"

"Yes!" Owen cries out in excitement. "Mom's going to love us in these."


## Ashley

Cameron sips his scotch, his sexy eyes locked on mine. "Don't look at me like that, Bloss, unless you're getting under the table and sucking my cock."

I raise my eyebrow and smile into my glass. It's Friday night —date night—and my man is in a very naughty mood.

He has that look in his eye... the one that I love.

We haven't talked about the wedding all week. I'm trying not to bring it up. I don't want to push him. Renovating the house is enough for me, and he has every right to have a say in where we have our wedding.

I'm thinking maybe his L.A. house is an option now. I really can't stand those pretentious wedding venues. I know he went and got his suit this week with the boys, and I miraculously found a dress.

It was the first one I tried on. Adrian lined up an exclusive appointment last night with a designer. Natasha and Jenna came with me. I didn't buy it because it *was* the first one... but I've been thinking about it all day.

It's classically feminine and I know that Cam will love it. Jenna and Natasha are going to be my bridesmaids. Everything is falling into place, with just the damn venue to sort out.

"We should get going," Cameron whispers as his dark eyes drop to my lips.

I glance at my watch. "It's early."

"Yes, but we have to leave early in the morning."

I frown. "Why? Where are we going tomorrow?"

He smiles sexily. "Pemberley."

My eyes widen. "Pemberley?"

He smirks and runs his finger back and forth over his sexy big lips as he watches me. I feel his seduction all the way to my sex. "Well, we do have a wedding to prepare for."

My mouth drops open. "You mean...?"

He smiles. "Yes, I mean." He picks up my hand and kisses the back of it. "Will you marry me at Pemberley, Ashley Tucker?"

I stare at him through tears and I nod. "Uh-huh."

"Six weeks," he says.

I frown. "Six weeks?"

"We get married in six weeks. The invitations have to go out this week."

"I-I don't think that's enough time, Cam," I stammer. "I won't be able to get time off work."

He runs his foot up my shin as his dark eyes hold mine. "I checked your schedule with Jameson and you can get six days off. The Friday before the wedding and then the week after for our honeymoon."

I watch him, half shocked. "We're going on a honeymoon?'

He smiles. "Yes, we're going on a honeymoon. Just because we are getting married in a barn it doesn't mean we don't get a week to ourselves."

I grin.

"And that's the only week I can do, Bloss. I have no major surgeries and I can reschedule everything else. Six weeks."

"But..." I frown. "But..." I shake my head. "There's so much to do. We won't have time. Pemberley is a disaster."

"I can handle it. I know you're snowed under. Adrian and I can handle it."

I smile softly. "Really?"

"Really." He thinks about it for a moment and then frowns. "Well, I hope."

I laugh.

His eyes hold mine and he licks his lips as he picks up my hand and kisses the palm. "And tonight, Miss Tucker, I want the best fucking head job you've ever given me."

I begin to feel my insides tingle as I watch him kiss me.

"What are you going to do with your cock in my mouth?" I whisper.

His eyes flash with arousal. "Blow the house down."

**Three weeks until the wedding**

I watch Cameron walk down the paddock with a huge piece of wood over his shoulder and I smile to myself. His little apprentice, Owen, is following him with a small piece of wood over his shoulder, too.

He idolizes his father... and so do I.

Cameron has worked his guts out every weekend to get this property ready for our wedding. His once-perfect hands are now covered in blisters.

Each night we've had a fire, roasted marshmallows, and then camped in the barn on our airbeds. I've fallen more in love with the place and what it represents by the hour. Although he hasn't openly admitted it I know Cameron is now attached, too. I overheard him talking about the property with pride in his voice to his doctor friend in the hospital cafeteria last week, telling him about the plans he has for the house. This weekend is the first weekend that we actually have nice bathrooms to use. They're finally done, and the fittings are all white marble with designer brass fittings. Cam organized the whole thing.

Unfortunately, upstairs has been ruled unsafe by the plumbers, so it's now a no-go zone and roped off. We'll tackle that nightmare after the wedding. I hear a truck in the distance. "It's here, boys," I call.

Owen and Cameron make their way back from the paddock, and we go out the front to meet the truck. Four hundred plants have arrived, as well as new turf. The man opens the back of the truck and my mouth drops open in shock. "Why...?" My eyes flick to Cameron. "That's... that's a ridiculous number of plants," I stammer.

Cameron frowns. "It does seem a lot, doesn't it?" His eyes flicker to me and he shrugs. "I don't know, that's just what the website said I needed."

"How many people have you got coming to help us plant these tomorrow?" I laugh.

"Well, Joshua and Natasha and the kids. Murph and Ben. Max, and two guards." He shrugs. "That's it." He frowns. "Who else can I ask?" he murmurs to himself.

I put my hand over my mouth and smile as the two men

unload our precious plants from the back of the truck. "We'll get it done." I smile. The funny thing is, because I'm so adamant that we are doing this ourselves, everyone seems to have caught the renovation bug. Joshua and Natasha came out last weekend, and Natasha helped me clean the barn while Joshua and Cameron mended and painted fences. I know that Adrian came out with Cam during the week for some of the planning, too. I had to laugh. Cam told me that, on the drive home, Adrian was writing to-do lists and got so stressed out with what had to be done that Cam had to pull into a bar and get him half-drunk just to relax him.

Cameron begins to help unpack the truck and I watch him for a moment. He's in grey designer sweat pants that are now covered in white paint, and a white Ralph Lauren shirt that's ripped across the shoulder from where he got caught on a nail earlier. His big work boots are scuffed and dirty. Owen is covered in mud and is wearing odd clothes that, only six weeks ago, his father would have died if he saw him in. Cameron's hair is crazy wild. Curls get the girls...

*Oh, they most certainly do.*

I take two of the plants and put them into the row with the others. Let's get this done.

———

It's the Wednesday before the wedding and I'm in the corridor of the hospital checking on a patient. I catch sight of my beloved husband-to-be doing his rounds with his group of interns.

My heart somersaults in my chest. He still makes my stomach flutter.

He's in his navy suit with a crisp white shirt and grey tie, and his hair in styled in that dark, messy look of perfection he rocks so well. His large, muscular body is the want of every nurse in the hospital. Everything about him screams power... *and he's all mine.*

They come around the corner and Cam smiles sexily. "Here she is, the lovely Ashley Tucker."

"Hello, Ashley." The interns all smile. "Good luck this weekend," one of them says.

"She doesn't need luck," Cameron replies calmly. "She's marrying me." He runs his hand down his tie and raises his eyebrow. "No luck required."

The interns all laugh, and I smirk. "Thank you," I reply to the intern who wished me well. "Although, I think I'll take your luck." I widen my eyes. "I'm going to need it."

They laugh again.

"I'm just doing my final rounds and then I'm off." He smiles.

I melt.

Cameron has taken the rest of the week off to go to Pemberley with Joshua and Adrian to prepare for Saturday. Adrian has been there all week in all his wedding-planning glory.

God knows what they have in store for us, but Cameron does seem pretty damn pleased with himself.

I've never seen him so excited. There have been secret phone calls to Adrian and Joshua which I'm not allowed to listen in on, plus folders of pictures of things that he keeps in his locked office drawer.

If all those women who knew the former player version of Cameron Stanton could see him now, absolutely thrilled to bits about planning his own wedding, what would they think?

*Who knew?*

I don't think he ever imagined being like this. I know I definitely couldn't have predicted it. Although his control-freak tendencies are being appeased, as he's getting to choose exactly what he wants.

I don't care what's in the barn.

As long as he, Owen, and the minister are there, the rest is just semantics.

He can have whatever the hell he wants.

## The Wedding Day - 2 p.m.

I exhale deeply as I look at my reflection in the mirror. My honey-blonde hair is down and has been curled into soft waves. My dress is off-the-shoulder and made from white lace, with long sleeves and a fitted bodice, plus a wide satin sash and a full organza skirt.

It's white.

I never thought I would wear white to my wedding, but I'm marrying my first love, so I figure it's fitting.

This dress is over the top, a fairy tale dress. But you know what? This is my fucking fairy tale and I'm inhaling every second of it.

I'm wearing a veil, and my makeup is gorgeous. She's one hell of a makeup lady that we hired.

Natasha is beaming when she walks into the room and takes my hand. I turn to my mother, who has tears in her eyes. "Jenna," she calls out. "She's ready."

Jenna walks in and her jaw drops in awe. "Oh, Ash, you look so beautiful," she whispers.

I tear up and turn back to the mirror to look at my reflection as my hands run down my ribcage.

"You ready to get married, babe?" Natasha whispers.

I smile at my reflection. "You bet I am. Let's go."

# CHAPTER 7

**Ashley**

THE STRETCH LIMOUSINE pulls in to the tree-lined driveway of Pemberley where cars are strategically parked in lines on the front paddock. I feel my nerves dance in my stomach.

"I hope everything's okay," I whisper. For the first time since coming up with the idea, I feel anxious about the farm meeting everyone's expectations. God, this could be a real disaster.

Poor Cameron. What was I thinking putting him under so much pressure?

I imagine Adrian, Joshua, and Cam racing to beat the clock through the week to get everything done in time, and I smile to myself. They've been working so hard.

The place looks amazing.

White organza sprays hang sporadically from the oak trees. The lawns are all freshly mowed, and the fences have been painted a crisp white.

Gardenias line the driveway, and a white screen has been put around the house to block it from view. Huge palm trees sit in pots along the screen to blend it into the surrounding greenery.

I knew he would cover up the house.

This place looks just like one of the swanky places that Cameron liked, only it's actually a hundred times better.

I catch sight of Adrian and Joshua standing outside the barn, and I smile as the car comes to a halt. Adrian is in a navy suit and Joshua is in his best-man attire.

Joshua looks up, and smiles as he waves to the car.

"Look at that hotty." Tash sighs as she sees her man. "Meow."

"Thanks for loaning Joshua to us for the week," I whisper as I take her hand in mine.

"Looks like they've been busy," she says as she looks around.

"Holy crap," Jenna whispers. "This place looks amazing. Poor bastards must have worked their fingers to the bone."

We all giggle.

The people start to buzz around, and I can hear someone yell in the distance, "Everyone into the hall. The bride has arrived."

My heart starts to thump.

"This is it, baby girl." My dad smiles as he picks up my hand and kisses the back of it.

I blow out a deep breath. "Gosh, I just want the formal part over with. I'm so nervous to walk in front of everyone." I put my hand on my stomach. "What if I trip or something?"

Tash smiles sympathetically. "You won't. Relax."

The car door opens, and the photographer appears. He starts to snap away, and I smile and try my hardest to look calm while my insides are jumping around in nervous anticipation.

I'm marrying Cameron...

In minutes.

My heart is overwhelmed with emotion as I smile for the camera.

He keeps clicking, clicking, and clicking, and finally I can't take it anymore. "That's enough." I smile. "I'm getting married now."

I climb out of the car and glance at my two bridesmaids. They're wearing a simple version of my dress, only in a pale lemon. They have capped sleeves, with a lace bodice and an organza skirt, although theirs aren't as full as mine. I wanted something timeless, that I could look back at photos in fifty years and still love.

I look down toward the hall and I smile. A blue stone path has been laid that leads all the way from the car to the barn. White flowers are planted on either side of the pathway and there's a white timber arch that's covered with white and lemon roses.

*Oh, this is so special.*

*Don't cry. Don't you dare cry!*

I'm not going to be one of those crazy chicks who sobs down the aisle. Or am I?

Please, God, no.

Tash hands me my flowers—an arrangement of white and lemon flowers that Owen helped me pick out—and I exhale deeply. "This is it," I whisper.

Natasha and Jenna beam with happiness before they both kiss me on the cheek.

"You ready?" one of the ushers asks.

I nod. "As ready as I'll ever be."

The usher nods to someone down at the barn, and moments later piano music starts to play. It's the Bridal March. I smile when I get a vision of Cam and Adrian picking out this song.

*Oh, I love this man.*

Natasha walks down the blue stone path first, with Jenna slowly following behind. I blow out a breath and link my arm through my father's.

"You look beautiful, baby girl." He smiles as he kisses my forehead.

"Thanks, Dad," I whisper as I choke up.

We begin to make our way down the path toward our hall. My heart is somersaulting hard in my chest. Every step feels like a mile and I want to run.

I want to run as fast as I can into Cameron's arms.

We get to the double doors at the back. The guests are all standing and watching, waiting for me to arrive.

*Oh my God. Oh my God.*

I look up the aisle of red carpet and there, at the end, he stands.

His hands are linked in front of him and he smiles sexily as he sees me. I feel myself melt.

He's wearing a black suit and bowtie. I've never seen a man look more beautiful than he does, and a broad smile takes over my face. Owen gets excited to see me, and Cameron reaches down to pick him up in his arms.

They both watch me in awe.

We slowly walk towards my two boys.

Cameron smiles softly as he watches me, desperately trying to keep his emotions under control and failing miserably.

His eyes are filled with tears.

I finally reach them, and Cam places Owen back down beside him. My father shakes Cameron's hand and passes my hand over to him. As if he can't control himself, Cameron leans in and kisses me softly, cupping my face. I smile up at him and he stares down at me lovingly.

We haven't seen each other for three long days.

"Is someone getting this on camera?" Carson calls jovially.

The crowd laughs.

"You getting soppy on me, Stanton?" I whisper.

He raises a brow. "Possibly."

He takes my hands in his and we face each other.

Our eyes are locked and while he fights tears, I'm fighting a goofy smile.

I don't really hear anything the minister says or take notice of anyone else in the barn; I don't even know what it looks like.

Because all I can see is him.

Looking at me, his eyes are filled with love.

This beautiful man. My knight in shining armor.

I'm snapped out of my daydream when the minister speaks to Cameron.

"Repeat after me."

I hold my breath.

"I, Cameron John Stanton, take you, Ashley Rose Tucker, to be my lawfully wedded wife. To have and to hold, from this day forward, for better for worse, for richer for poorer, in sickness and in health, until death do us part." He smiles as he slides the ring onto my finger and I smile back, bouncing on the spot a little.

The crowd giggles.

Now it's my turn.

"I, Ashley Rose Tucker, take you, Cameron John Stanton, to be my lawfully wedded husband. To have and to hold, from this day forward, for better for worse, for richer for poorer, in sickness and in health, until death us do part." I concentrate as I slide the gold band onto Cameron's finger.

"I now pronounce you husband and wife. You may kiss your bride."

We both laugh, and Cam grabs my face and kisses me softly. It's a wedding kiss. We practiced this... a *lot*.

A little bit of suction, a little bit of tongue, and a whole lot of perfect.

The crowd cheers as we kiss. Owen bangs Cameron on the leg, feeling left out. Cam bends down and picks him up, and the three of us put our arms around each other.

*My family is united.*

———

I walk around the beautiful wedding reception in wonder. I can't believe this place.

How the hell has Cam pulled this off?

The barn has been transformed into an amazing reception hall, with large circular tables that are covered in fresh flowers and candles. A piano and a violin play up in the back corner. Outside is like a scene from a movie. The big oak tree's branches are all covered in fairy lights. Large white seats have been strategically placed all around, and there's a cocktail bar where a server is making the most delicious- looking cocktails that I have ever seen. Fire lanterns are lit around the perimeter, and waitresses are circling with champagne and canapés. Our family and friends are all here.

I feel two hands snake around my hips and then soft lips press against my ear.

"Hello, Mrs. Stanton." Cameron smiles against me.

I laugh and turn in his arms. "Cam, this is so beautiful. Thank you so much." I kiss him softly and look around in awe. "It's absolutely perfect."

Adrian walks over to stand with us.

"Thank you so much, Adrian. This is amazing," I whisper. "More beautiful than anything I've ever seen."

Adrian kisses my cheek, glances around, and lifts his chin proudly. "It is, isn't it?"

I see a speck of white paint in Cam's hair and I giggle as I tuck the piece behind his ear.

"You have paint in your hair." I smile.

"You have no idea," he mutters dryly as he glances at Adrian. "This was hardcore. We should have filmed it for some reality television show."

Adrian raises his eyebrows. "It really was. I thought I was going to die yesterday. We're lucky to still be here. But at least you can take your hands out of your pockets."

I frown in question and he pulls his hands out. His cuticles have white paint imbedded on them. My mouth falls open in shock and I burst out laughing.

"We ran out of time and turpentine," Adrian mutters dryly. "It's appalling."

"Did you see Stan's legs?" Cameron laughs.

"Oh no." I laugh as I put my hand over my mouth. "What's wrong with Joshua's legs."

"Covered in paint," Cameron replies. "But I got the last of the turpentine because I was the one getting married. We sent someone to get some more but it was too late; the photographers arrived before they got back."

My heart melts and I put my arms around them both. "It means so much to me that you did everything here yourselves." I tear up.

"Now she cries," Cameron replies flatly with an eye roll. "She marries the greatest man on Earth and sheds not a tear. The minute she finds out we're covered in paint and *boom*."

"I'm about to curl into a fetal position and cry about this paint, too," Adrian says flatly as he looks at his fingernails.

We all laugh and Adrian glances at his watch. "The cake and speeches are in five minutes." We watch him walk off through the crowd as he immediately snaps back into his wedding-planner role, and I slide my arms around my husband.

"Thank you so much, Cam." I kiss him softly. "You have no idea how much this means to me."

His lips linger on mine. "Yes, I do. That's why I did it."

"I love you," I whisper.

"You'd better." He smiles down at me. "Let's go cut our wedding cake."

---

We've cut the cake, my father and Joshua have given their speeches and toasts, and the teaspoons have started to hit the champagne glasses. Everyone is waiting for his speech.

Cameron rolls his lips nervously and stands.

Owen comes and sits on my lap, looking up at his father.

Cam puts his hand on the top of his affectionately as he gathers his thoughts.

Joshua hands him the microphone and Cam exhales heavily. *Oh, he's nervous.*

I smile as I watch him.

"I would like to thank you all for coming today. We know it was a long trek, but Ashley and I really appreciate it." He turns to Joshua and Adrian, who are sitting on the other side of him. "To my two best men." He watches them for a moment and then scrunches his lips together as he becomes emotional, dropping his head.

Joshua shakes his head and Adrian smiles proudly as he watches on.

"I'm trading you both in for new best friends as soon as possible." Cam frowns as he regains composure. "Out with the old and in with the new is my new mantra."

The crowd bursts into laughter. It's such a Cameron thing to say.

He puts his hand on Joshua's shoulder. "On a serious note..." He pauses and swallows the lump in his throat. "Thank you both for always being there for me." He drops his head again, unable to speak through emotion, and I smile through tears.

"Fucking pussy," Joshua whispers up at him with a smirk.

Cameron shakes his head as he desperately tries to regain his composure.

He turns his attention to me and smiles softly. "Ashley. My beautiful wife."

The crowd smiles and cheers, and he takes a sip of his beer and then he holds it up to offer a silent toast.

He frowns as he thinks. "I had this big three-page speech written out for you." He frowns. "But there aren't any words to describe what I feel." He frowns again and swallows.

My eyes tear up even more. He's really struggling here.

He smiles and looks at the guests. "You all know our story. We met in Vegas and I fell hopelessly in love with her." He puts his hand over his heart to accentuate his point.

The crowd laughs.

"I lost my phone and had no way of finding her, so the next weekend I went to New York, desperately hoping that I would find this woman who was haunting my every thought."

The crowd gushes, and I smile.

*I love this story.*

"I even put an ad in the classifieds to try to find her." He smiles down at me and I take his hand to kiss it. "But..." He smiles cheekily. "Much to my surprise, she didn't want to find me back." He widens his eyes and holds his hand out. "I know. Shocking, isn't it?"

"She was dodging a bullet," Carsen calls, and everyone laughs.

He takes my hand in his and I smile up at him. "And then fate stepped in and gave her a transfer across the country to be one of my interns. You can imagine my surprise when my dream girl walked through those hospital doors and into my office all those years later."

His face falls serious and he drops his head. "And I met this perfect little version of myself." He rubs our son's head. "His name is Owen."

Owen smiles proudly up at his father and my vision becomes blurred.

Cam frowns as he tries to articulate his thoughts. "You know... I thought I was happy. I thought I had it all figured out. That was, until Ashley walked back into my life with Owen and I found out what true happiness really was." He smiles down at me. "Suddenly nothing else mattered anymore. She and Owen became my everything."

The crowd swoons.

He looks down at me. "I love you, Ashley." He bends to kiss me softly and I smile against his lips. He stands and raises his glass in the air. "To Mrs. Stanton, and the best son in the world," he calls.

Owen's eyes light up with excitement.

The crowd stands to clap and cheer. "To Mrs. Stanton, and the best son in the world."

A song starts and Cameron smiles, taking my hand in his.

"Dance with me, Bloss?"

I stand, and he leads me out onto the dancefloor, taking me into his arms as the iconic melody rings out.

> *"Wise men say only fools rush in,*
> *But I can't help falling in love with you."*

I hear the song and break into a beaming grin. "Elvis?" I ask.

"The king for my queen." He smiles and kisses me softly as we sway to the music.

Suddenly, we're alone in the room. I can't see anything or anyone else but him.

"We did it." I run my fingers down his cheekbone as I study his perfect face. "We actually got married, Cam."

He spins me around super-fast and we lose our footing, nearly falling over. I laugh out loud. "You're a terrible dancer."

He raises a cheeky brow. "You have no idea what you're talking about, Bloss." He spins me again.

"Yes, I do." I now know where the term *drunk on love* comes from. I feel like I'm going to overdose on love here. I'm on a Cameron Stanton high. "I'm the luckiest girl in the world," I whisper up at him.

His mischievous eyes hold mine. "That's true. You are." He winks. "I will undoubtedly be the best husband of all time." He twirls me again, and we nearly fall over once more.

I laugh into his chest.

"I'm taking you home, Mrs. Stanton," he whispers into my ear with that devilish tone in his voice. "I'm ready to start the rest of my life with my wife." He pauses for a moment. "Hey. That rhymes." He raises his brows. "See that? Now that I'm married, I'm just making up poems naturally. This stuff is just rolling off my tongue. This is definitely going to raise my romance score. You are one lucky woman."

I roll my eyes and giggle. "Give me an hour." I kiss him softly. "I want to see everyone before we leave."

Owen taps Cameron on the leg and Cam lifts him up to dance with us. He spins us around and Owen squeals in delight. "Nearly bedtime, buddy." Cam smiles as he kisses his head. Owen nods an over-exaggerated nod and rubs his little eyes.

"Where are we staying, anyway?" I ask.

Cameron shrugs. "Some dumpy hotel down the road. I don't know, I haven't seen it yet."

I giggle.

Owen's face falls as he looks between us. "What about me?" He's exhausted and fragile. "Can I come to dumpy?" he whispers in his little worried voice.

"Yeah. You, too. We can't leave you out of dumpy. You're the dumpy king." Cam tickles Owen's ribs, and he chuckles as he tries to wriggle away.

I frown.

Cam shrugs. "I want Owen to be near us on our first night as a real family." He kisses me quickly. "In another room, don't worry," he mouths.

Owen puts his head down on his father's shoulder in relief.

I smile broadly and kiss him softly. "This is why I love you."

He leans his head against mine and smiles. "We need to leave soon, Bloss, or you're going to find Owen and me asleep in the car. This wedding shit is exhausting."

I laugh. "Okay, half an hour it is."

———

An hour and a half later we say our final goodbyes to our circle of friends and climb into the back of the limo. Everyone is laughing and cheering as the driver pulls out, and the car rattles and clangs from the tin cans tied to the back of it.

"Here we go." I smile as I wave to our guests through the window. The car slowly pulls out of the driveway, up around the corner, and out of view from everyone at the wedding, and then the car stops.

I frown. "What's he doing?"

Cam shrugs. "I don't know."

The door opens, and the driver holds out his hand. "We've arrived at your destination, Mr. and Mr. Stanton," he says.

Huh? I look over to Cameron and he's smiling like a Cheshire cat. "Cam?" I frown. "What's going on?"

He kisses me quickly. "Owen and I have got a surprise for you, Bloss."

My eyes flicker to the house in front of us.

"Get out of the car." He smiles.

"Oh." I shuffle across and climb out of the car to get out, and he opens the white gate in the screen.

Oh, my God. My hands fly to my mouth. The front veranda has been refloored and the weatherboards have been freshly painted white. "You painted this?" I gasp.

Cam shakes his head. "We started it, but we ran out of time." He pulls me to the front door and opens it. I peer in. Everything is sheeted off, but the stairs have been re-timbered.

My eyes widen. "You started the house?" I whisper.

Cameron smiles, and with his sleepy son on his hip he leads me up the stairs by the hand. On our arrival upstairs, I peer down the hall to see a light coming out of the master suite. A large red bow is stuck to the door.

Cameron proudly leads me down the hall and opens the bedroom door.

My mouth falls open and my wide eyes flicker to him in shock. The bedroom is finished... and not *just* finished, but it's completely amazing.

"What?" I look around, but I don't know where to look first.

"Cameron..." I whisper. Tears instantly fill my eyes. I'm surrounded by beautiful cream walls and a plush carpet, and he's fitted coffee-colored drapes to hang over the windows. I stare up at the light. "A chandelier," I whisper.

A huge king-size bed with padded headboard sits against the wall, the same colors as the drapes. There are two beautiful wingback chairs and ottomans near the window, too.

"You did this?" I whisper. "You did this for me?"

"Yes."

My tears flow over and run down my cheeks.

"Oh, there's more." Cam smiles as he opens a door. "A beautiful cream marble bathroom, too."

"Cameron..." I whisper. I look around at the perfect room and frown. "How could you have possibly done this?"

"A lot of bickering between Stan, Murph, and me," he replies dryly.

I laugh as I imagine the three of them here this week working like slaves.

"You did all this?" I whisper.

He nods. "The builder knocked out one of the adjacent bedrooms to make room for the bathroom and walk-in closet, and then the bathroom and plastering we had done professionally, but we did everything else." He looks around and smiles proudly. "I wanted our first night together as man and wife to be somewhere special." His eyes search mine. "Do you like it, baby?"

I kiss his lips tenderly. "Oh, I love it. I love you." I grab him and squeeze him tight. "Thank you, thank you."

"Oh, and we did your room a little, Owie. But it's not finished yet." He leads us to the closest bedroom and opens it. I smile broadly. The room is plastered, and one lone, single bed sits in the middle.

"We didn't have time to paint it yet." He shrugs.

I wrap my arms around his neck and start to kiss him all over his face. "I love you."

Cameron smiles and kisses my neck. "Bed, big boy." He smiles to his son.

Owen is half-asleep when Cam lies him down and takes his shoes off before he covers him over. We sit on the bottom of the bed for a moment until he falls asleep fully, and then we tiptoe out.

Cameron carefully closes our bedroom door and clicks the lock. His eyes rise to mine.

My heart somersaults in my chest.

"All I could think about all night is taking this dress off you," he whispers as he comes to me. His lips take mine; his tongue slowly sweeps between my lips as his hand holds my jaw in place. "Do you know how fucking beautiful you looked today?" He drops his lips to my neck and he bites me hard.

Goosebumps scatter up my arms and I close my eyes in pleasure. "You are so perfect," he growls.

My eyes flicker to the door. "Is the door locked, Cam?

"Yes." He nibbles my neck as his hands drop to my behind.

I step back and kneel before him. His eyes flicker with arousal. I begin to unzip his suit pants and I look up at him. "I want to suck my new husband's cock in my wedding dress," I whisper as I kiss him through his boxers.

He smiles sexily as his eyes hold mine. "Fuck, yeah." He

brushes the hair back from my forehead tenderly as he watches me.

I pull down his briefs and am gifted with a perfect sight. Pre-ejaculate is beading on the end, and I slowly lick it off.

He inhales sharply.

I take him deep and he closes his eyes. I feel his knees go weak as he puts his hand on the back of the wingback chair to steady himself.

I take him deeper and deeper, my hand following my tongue as I pump him with force.

"Oh, my God," he moans. "That's so fucking good." He tips his head back and pants as I give him a good going-over. He's put in all this work for me and now I'm going to put all my work in for him.

"Ash..." he pants as his face scrunches tight. "I need a photo."

"What?" I whisper around his cock.

"I need a photo of you sucking my cock in your wedding dress."

"You're a deviant." I take him deep again. "Get your camera." I smile.

"Yes," he whispers. He holds the camera in place and, as I take him deep, I look at him and he takes the shot. He takes another, and then another, and then he drops the camera and watches me in awe. His eyes darken.

"I need to fuck my wife," he growls in a whisper.

I giggle. "Don't you mean *make love*? I think married people make love, Cameron," I tease.

He shakes his head as he pulls me to my feet and turns me away from him. He slowly slides the zipper down.

"Nope. No making love in this fucking house," he whispers as his lips dust my neck. He slides my dress down from behind and hisses when he sees my white wedding lingerie: a white bra and corset, with a matching g-string and garter belt. My stockings are thigh-high and white.

His eyes drop down my body and rest on my sex before they travel back up to my face. "If you married me for romance, Mrs. Stanton, I'm afraid you will be sadly disappointed." He trails his finger down between my breasts and then down to my sex. He rubs me in small circles through my panties, and then he cups my sex aggressively with his whole hand, gripping me tight.

"This body is mine now," he purrs. He slides my panties to the side and impales me with three fingers.

"Ahh..." I moan as I throw my head back.

"We won't be making love, Ashley." He pumps me hard with his thick fingers, and my eyes close. "We're going to be fucking hard. Day and night, night and day."

He bites my neck aggressively and my legs nearly give way.

He pulls his pants down and lies back on the bed. "Get on me and ride this cock."

I go to remove my bra and he holds his hand up in a stop gesture.

"I want the underwear and veil left on." He licks his lips as his eyes drop to my sex. "Tonight, I get to fuck my wife."

# CHAPTER 8

**Ashley**

THE PITTER-PATTER of little feet wakes me from my slumber, and I inhale deeply. It's early morning and the sun is just peeking through the drapes.

"Dad," Owen says into the silence.

Cameron stays sleeping.

"Dad," he calls again.

"Hmm." Cameron frowns and pulls the blankets back. His son climbs into his arms and Cam kisses the top of his head. "Go back to sleep, buddy," he whispers groggily.

I smile and put my arm over Cameron and dust the back of my fingers down Owen's face. "Good morning, my beautiful Owie," I mumble, smiling sleepily.

"Morning, Momma," he whispers in his husky little voice.

We lie in silence for another half hour.

"Dad, I'm hungry." Owen stretches.

Cameron's eyes stay shut. "Sshh," he whispers with his eyes still shut. "Don't wake Momma; she's very tired."

"Mom's already awake," Owen replies, annoyed.

"Huh?" Cameron rolls over and smiles when he sees me with my eyes open. "Well, well, well. If it isn't Mrs. Stanton in the flesh." He slides his hand around my waist and kisses me softly. "I thought you were still asleep." He smiles.

"No, I was letting you sleep in."

He smiles against my lips, as if remembering something. "We got married yesterday."

I laugh. "Huh, fancy that. We did." I get up and throw my robe on and open the drapes and look around my beautiful room. There's even a framed photograph of the three of us on my bedside table. "I just love this room, Cam." I shake my head. "I love everything about it. What you picked, how you did it. The fact that you did it yourself."

Cam smiles proudly as he looks around. "Hmm, me too."

I smirk; I would just love to tease him about loving this room...but, I won't.

"How did you ever pull this off?" I ask.

"With great difficulty," he sighs, his eyes still closed.

"Dad, I'm really hungry." Owen frowns. "Get up."

Cameron is the one who usually fusses over Owen in the mornings. However, today, the poor man is exhausted.

"Daddy is tired, baby. I'll get your breakfast," I reply.

Cameron yawns. "It's not here yet; I have to ring for it."

"Huh?" I frown.

"The hotel down the road is bringing up a full breakfast out in the garden, but I have to ring for it." He yawns sleepily. "I couldn't cook you anything because we don't have a kitchen yet."

Owen's eyes widen in horror; he's getting hangry. "Well, how long will that be?"

"I packed some Muesli bars and bananas in your backpack, Owen," Cam replies.

"Come on, let's go get your backpack until breakfast arrives." I smile.

Cameron gets up and sleepily pulls his boxers on.

"Stay in bed, Cam," I say.

"Hmm, no." He looks out the window. "I've got to put the sprinklers on our plants."

"What?" I frown.

"We won't be back for a week and I'm worried they're going to die." He sighs. "We do go on our honeymoon this afternoon, remember?" He shakes his head at my forgetfulness.

"Am I coming on the moon-honey?" Owen asks.

"No. Remember you're going to stay with Blake and Natasha and Joshua," Cameron says. "We're bringing you back a big present." He widens his eyes to accentuate his point. "Huge."

Owen smiles. "Oh, yeah, that's right. Sick." He punches the air in excitement.

Cameron looks out the window. "I'll need to give the garden a good soaking, though, now. We'll leave in three hours, okay?"

I drop my head and smile at the floor. "Is that a garden attachment I'm picking up on, Dr. Stanton?" I tease.

His eyes glance up to me and he smirks, knowing full well I've got him.

"Well..." His eyes flick back outside again. "I didn't want to put all that work in for nothing," he replies matter-of-factly.

I fold my arms in front of me as I lean up against the wall. "Who knew that Cameron Stanton would trade nightclubs for gardening?"

His eyes dance with mischief. "I'll be sowing a few more seeds this week for that matter."

My eyes hold his. "If you're lucky."

"No luck required," he fires back. "I have a wife now. I can do whatever the hell I want with her."

I smile. "Is that so?"

He holds up his hand and shows me the gold band on his finger with a raised eyebrow, and I smile broadly. "That is one sexy hand."

He takes me in his arms. "Well, I have one sexy wife."

"Eww. Stop kissing. I just want a banana," Owen snaps.

"Owen." Cameron sighs, losing his patience. "I want to give your mother a banana. Go and find the backpack please. Now."

Owen scowls and heads into his room in search of his backpack, and Cameron kisses me. Deep, aggressive tongue as he grips the back of my head. Dominant perfection, my whole body tingles.

"I can't wait to get you on your own for a week," he whispers darkly, pulling my bottom lip out with his teeth and nipping it hard.

I jump at the sting. He then leaves the room and I watch the doorway he just left through. My body thumps with arousal from his momentary touch.

A week alone with my husband...and the mood he's in... I think I should be scared.

———

I smile sleepily as I lean my head on Cam's shoulder. We're on a plane en-route to our honeymoon in Paris...another surprise.

Cameron is doing a crossword and I know he's trying to calm his nerves about leaving Owen; he's never had to do it before. I thought he was going to call the whole thing off when Owen got teary as we left.

"He'll be fine, Cam," I sigh.

Cam nods as he pretends to concentrate on the crossword. "I know," he replies. "Maybe he would have been better staying with Jenna?"

"He's staying with Jenna through the day, but you said you wanted him to stay with Tash at night because she has guards with her all the time," I reply.

"I know." He flicks his pen as he thinks.

"It's one week."

He nods. "I know."

I smile as I watch him. "And he's crawled into bed with Tash and Josh before in the middle of the night, they don't mind." I smile softly. "He's in very safe hands."

"A week's a long time to a little kid," he murmurs.

"Cameron, he'll be fine," I reassure him. "He gets to spend time with his cousins, and this is the first week we have been away alone together. Ever."

He frowns. "We went to New York."

"Yes. And I was sick with nerves the whole time, knowing that you were going to leave me any second."

His brow creases. "How the hell did you do this parent thing on your own?"

I shrug. "It was hard." I think for a moment. "But not as hard as knowing that one day Owen was going to ask me who his father was." I narrow my eyes as I think. "And knowing I couldn't tell him the answer because I didn't even know."

Cam shakes his head. "Fuck, Ash. What a nightmare that would have been."

I smile sadly as I think. "You know, I look back to when

Owen was a baby, and even my pregnancy, and I feel like..." I pause.

"You feel like what?" he asks.

"I feel like I didn't even enjoy being pregnant, you know? I was so scared and constantly worried about money and med school."

Cam's face falls and he puts his arm around me and kisses my forehead. "Next pregnancy will be different, Bloss. I promise."

I smile and then I frown.

"What?" he asks.

"When do you think we could have another baby, Cam?"

He frowns. "I thought you would want to wait a while. I didn't want to bring it up and make you feel pressured," he replies.

"Owen will be five soon and if we want more," I shrug, "I'm afraid the age gap will be too big between him and his brothers or sisters and then they won't be close."

"Whenever you want, baby." He smiles up against my face as he holds me close. "I'm happy with the family I've already got, but if it were up to me I would be trying to get you pregnant on this trip. I'm going to practice anyway, of course," he mutters.

I look up at him in shock. "What? A baby now? Really?"

"We could?" He purses his lips as he thinks. "But... I know how much you gave up to have Owen, so the decision on when is yours. When you're ready is when it will happen."

I smile against his chest. "How many children do you want, Cameron?" It feels funny to be talking about this.

"Twelve," he replies without hesitation.

"Twelve?" I laugh. "That's not happening, I can tell you right now."

"Okay, six."

"Six?" I shake my head. "Are you drunk?"

Cameron smiles and kisses my lips. "Drunk on you."

"Cam." I shake my head. "Babies are messes and crying and sleepless nights."

He smiles. "And if they give me the same kind of feeling that Owen gives me, then bring it the fuck on."

My eyes hold his. *I love this man.* "You know, Cameron, sometimes the things you say... and how hard you love me and Owen... you could probably get me pregnant just by looking at me if you really wanted to," I whisper.

"I like having sex with you too much to try that method," he replies dryly.

"You're an animal." I smile.

He picks up his pen and goes back to his crossword. "That would make you Mrs. Animal," he replies flatly as he reads. "Actually, put that on my headstone. Here lies Mr. Animal, husband to Mrs. Animal, who loved sucking cock." He raises an eyebrow. "Hmm, I like it."

I roll my eyes. "Do your crossword, idiot." I glance over his shoulder and read the next question. "Vostok 6," I murmur.

Camerons eyes flick up to me and he frowns and reads the question out loud. "In which craft did Valencia Tereshkova make her historic space flight?" He narrows his eyes at me. "How do you know that?"

I shrug. "I don't know. I must have read it once."

"Your brain is a real fucking turn on, you know?" He licks his lips. "You better watch out or I will get you pregnant."

Our eyes are locked.

"I dare you," I whisper.

"Dare is a strong word... I am a goal-orientated man, you know." He raises an eyebrow in question.

My eyes drop to his lips. "So I've heard."

He kisses me slowly. "Challenge accepted. My mission is now crystal clear. Fuck my brainiac wife and inject her with my super human sperm."

"Oh, my God." I laugh out loud. "You are determined on keeping that romance score as low as possible, aren't you?"

He winks sexily and sips his scotch. "You bet, baby."

———

We walk down the street, hand in hand.

This is the honeymoon of all honeymoons. I can't stop smiling. We have eaten and laughed our way around Paris. Sleeping in, having sex whenever we want, sleeping late, drinking cocktails, sightseeing, speaking French...when it's actually necessary.

"I love Paris." I smile.

"Paris loves you," Cam replies casually. "Let's go home and spend the afternoon in bed."

"That sounds awfully good."

His eyes flick to mine and he smiles darkly. "Do you want to stop for a few drinks before we go back to our hotel?"

"No," I reply as I look at the bustling street around us. "Let's just go home."

We walk past a pharmacy. "I've just got to go in here for a moment." He pulls me in by the hand.

I'm not really concentrating and I just follow him around. "What are you looking for?" I ask as he looks for something specific.

"I think it should be..." He frowns and goes to the next aisle and looks around. "Aha." He picks a large bottle off the shelf and then keeps looking for something, and then picks another bottle from the shelf.

"What's that?" I ask.

His eyes hold mine. "Lube."

What?

My eyes widen and I swallow the lump in my throat.

*Fuck.*

"Sure you don't want that drink?" he asks as he raises his brow.

"Yeah, maybe I will," I murmur.

"You should maybe have a few." His eyes drop to my lips. "You're going to need to relax. I need my wife soft and supple to work with."

*Double fuck.*

———

Two hours and a few cocktails later, we burst into our room. Cameron has been talking dirty to me for the last two hours and I'm pretty sure if he blows in my direction I'll orgasm. Our lips are locked and he walks me backwards.

"You know, Cam, I was thinking." He slides my jeans down my legs, completely preoccupied.

"Did it hurt?" he murmurs against my breast.

I fake a laugh. "You're so funny." I hold the top of his head as it drops lower, down my stomach.

"You know..." I pause as he bites my hip bone, and my mouth falls open. "I'm not really into this, Cameron."

He bites me hard.

"I like our sex life the way it is. I don't think I want to change it. You don't try and fix what isn't broken...right?"

He stands and his eyes hold mine. "This isn't up for discussion, Ashley." His voice has dropped to that dominant tone he gets when aroused.

I frown.

He runs his finger underneath my jaw and lifts my face so that it's only millimeters from his. "You're my wife."

I get goosebumps.

"And I want to fuck your beautiful ass."

I swallow the lump in my throat as a fission of fear runs through me.

"And I'm taking what's mine. Today."

I frown. "It's not that I don't want to but... you're really big, Cam," I whisper. "It scares me."

"Have I ever hurt you, Bloss?"

I shake my head. "No."

"You know I would never hurt you." He kisses me, hard lips and soft tongue, and I feel my arousal start to pump. "I love you." He kisses me again. "I want all of you." Our kisses turn desperate. "I want you to want to please me and give me what I need."

I can feel my body submitting to his.

"Trust me," he whispers against my lips.

Our kiss is slow and tender and perfect, and fuck I do want to give him this.

*It's our honeymoon.*

"What if it starts to hurt?"

"It *will* hurt... you know it will at first." He slides my top over my shoulders and throws it to the floor, and undoes my bra and throws it off, too. He sucks on my nipple, hard enough that I wince in pain. "But sometimes a bit of pain is so, so good," he murmurs against my skin.

I close my eyes as he drops to his knees in front of me and slides my skirt down, and then my panties.

I have my hands on his shoulders and he inhales deeply.

My eyes close in pleasure.

"You smell so fucking good, baby," he whispers. He lifts my leg so it's over his shoulder and licks my open flesh. He nibbles and licks and bites me, and I grip his shoulders as I try to remain standing. "Over to the bed, Bloss," he whispers.

My heart is thumping hard in my chest and he leads me by the hand. "Lie down," he whispers.

With his eyes not leaving mine, he lifts his t-shirt over his head.

My legs want to open by themselves, and I writhe in anticipation.

He slides his jeans down and then his briefs, and I am gifted with the sight of his huge hard penis that hangs heavily between his legs.

He starts to slowly stroke himself. "This is how it's going to go, Bloss. I'm going to warm you up. Then I'm going to lube you up."

I frown. "Yes," I whisper.

"Then I'm going to put you on your hands and knees."

I stare at him as my heart hammers in my chest. "Yes," I whisper.

"Then I'm going to lube you up again."

I can't breathe.

He strokes himself and my mouth goes dry... he's so hot.

"And you're going to beg me to fuck you."

I nod, no words will leave my mouth. I'm hardly breathing.

"Once I start, I'm not stopping."

My scared eyes hold his.

"Do you understand me, Ashley?"

I nod.

*Fuck.*

He comes and sits next to me on the bed, spreads my legs wide and runs his fingertips through the lips of my sex. "Such a pretty pussy," he whispers as he looks down at my open body.

I close my eyes and softly moan.

He slides in three fingers aggressively and I wince; he pumps me harder and harder and harder and I cry out as my back arches off the bed.

For ten minutes he rides me with his hard fingers until I can't see straight.

"Get on your hands and knees, baby. I need to taste you."

I frown. *What?*

"Do it," he growls.

I shuffle onto my hands and knees and he comes around behind me and spreads my legs wide. "Down onto your elbows, Bloss."

I drop down to my elbows and he puts his three fingers back into my sex.

In...out...in...out. Harder and harder and harder, and the bed is rocking, and I can't think as my body rides out the pleasure.

And then his tongue sears my back opening, and I drop my head to the mattress.

Oh, my fucking God...this is too much.

*Senses overload.*

His fingers pump me hard while his tongue laps at me tenderly. "Don't come," he growls.

*What?*

"Cam," I pant as my body lurches back and forward. "I'm going to come. I can't last."

He takes his fingers out and my body collapses onto the bed in a heap.

"Up on your knees!" he growls.

I get back up onto my knees and he begins to lick me again,

and my legs are shaking and I can't hold myself up. I can see him through my legs, and pre-ejaculate is dripping from his cock.

*He is so turned on.*

"Fuck me, Cameron," I whimper. "Fuck me now."

Satisfaction crosses his face and he stands and gets the lube, and pours it into his hand and begins to rub it all over my sex and behind.

He massages and massages and it feels so good, and then he slides his finger in deep and my eyes widen as my breath catches.

With one hand holding me by the shoulder, the other hand slowly begins to ride me.

I drop my head and moan.

In, out, and around and around.

I hate to admit it, but this feels—

"That's it, baby," he whispers. "Feels so good, doesn't it?"

I nod my head and I think I have double vision. My body begins to take him in a rhythm.

Oh.

My.

Fucking.

God.

Then I feel him nudge his cock at my entrance and I close my eyes. He grabs my hip with one hand and guides himself into me with the other.

Ah, fuck.

I screw up my face.

"Relax, baby," he whispers.

He shuffles my legs further apart.

"Relax, baby; I won't hurt you."

I nod and drop my head and try to relax myself, and he pushes forward hard and nails me to the bed.

Searing pain rips through me and I screw up my face into the mattress.

"Ash." He kisses my shoulder. "I'm in, baby." He kisses my back. "That's the worst of it." He bites my shoulder as I try to control my breathing. "Kiss me," he pleads. I turn my head and we kiss softly over my shoulder, and it's tender and beautiful.

"I love you," he whispers.

I smile against his lips. "You'd better."

He chuckles. "I'm going to move, Bloss." He rubs my hips as he slowly pulls out and slides back home. He pours some oil over my behind and down onto the place where our bodies join. "Fuck," he moans. "This is something else." He slides out slowly and the oil releases some of the pressure, and he slides home easily this time.

He reaches around and starts to circle over my oily clitoris with his fingertips as he pulls out again and my body quivers. "Oh, you like that," he whispers in my ear from behind. "My beautiful wife loves getting filled with my cock. Do you have any idea how fucking hot you look right now?" he moans. He pumps me with force and I cry out. With one hand on my hipbone manouvering my angle and the two fingers deep within my sex, he starts to ride me hard.

My eyes are rolled back in my head.

I've never felt something so fucking good.

Deep...so deep.

And surprisingly intimate. This isn't at all what I expected.

Our skin is slapping hard. He grabs a handful of my hair and rips my head back, so he can kiss me over his shoulder. He pulls me aggressively up onto his lap and I'm putty in his dominant hands.

He's everywhere, in my mouth, in my sex, in my ass. His hand reaches around and he squeezes my nipple and that's it, I can't take anymore. I convulse into an orgasm.

"Fuck!" he yells and then he lifts me and slams me repeatedly down onto him. "Fuck, fuck, fuck." He holds himself deep and his body jerks as it explodes.

He drops his head to my shoulder and we both pant. we're covered in a sheen of perspiration and are both struggling to catch our breath.

He starts to trail soft kisses up my neck as he silently thanks me for letting him have what he needed.

I smile as I lie back on his body. "I think you just impregnated a lady downstairs in the lobby," I pant.

I feel him smile above me. "I think so." We kiss softly. "You are amazing." He kisses me softly again. "You all right?" he whispers as he studies my face.

"I know. I am pretty amazing." I kiss him again as I pant. "It was worth getting married for, I suppose."

He laughs and picks me up and throws me onto the bed. "Shut up or I'll do it again."

# CHAPTER 9

**Ashley**

**18 months later**

I INHALE DEEPLY AND SMILE.

"What are you smiling at, Tucker?" Cam raises his brow.

"Nothing." I shrug. "Stupidly happy."

Cameron sips his red wine and smiles sexily. "Well, you just finished work today—I can't imagine how that feels. Congratulations."

I rub my two hands over my heavily pregnant stomach and Cameron's eyes watch me and then rise to my lips. "Do you have any fucking idea how beautiful you are pregnant?" he whispers darkly.

Goosebumps run down my arms. "I thought you liked my body before."

His tongue darts out and licks his bottom lip. "I did." He

pauses as his eyes hold mine. "But this..." He frowns as he tries to articulate. "But this new body of yours is a whole other level of arousal. I seriously can't get fucking enough."

"You better take me home then, big boy," I whisper.

It's date night and things have been dreamy over the last eighteen months.

I finished my medical degree and have been working full time at the hospital. Owen started at his snooty private school and I hate to admit it...but it's an amazing school and he's really loving it. He's made some lovely little friends.

Jenna moved in with her boyfriend from next door and she's as happy as can be.

And me...well...I'm still drunk on Cameron Stanton...my husband.

Things have only gotten better for the two of us, if that's possible.

It took us nearly a year to get pregnant and I was secretly beginning to worry a little. When it finally did happen, and I got to tell Cameron, he stared at the pregnancy test for two hours, in shock. It suddenly became very real.

Pemberley is half-finished. We go there most weekends but there's only so much you can do in one full day a week.

The new kitchen is in, and Owen's bedroom and most of the living areas are finished. We are now working on the remaining bedrooms, but we haven't been able to go for a few weeks now and won't again until after the baby arrives. It's too far away from my obstetrician, and Cameron is silently freaking out.

I'm due in four weeks and am huge. No cute little belly for me—I am pregnant in all my glory.

Thankfully, Cameron has been worshipping the very ground I walk on. It's like he's trying to make up for missing out on my pregnancy with Owen.

He finishes his drink. "Let's go then, Bloss. I've got plans for you." He stands and takes my hand, and I waddle my way over to the elevator in my tight black dress.

He glances over at me and I drop my head.

*Here we go.*

The doors open. Three middle-aged women are at the back and a young man is to the side. We walk in and turn to face the doors.

He smirks at the floor as his latest skit comes to him, and then looks up and gets all serious as he concentrates on his task.

"Please don't tell my wife that I got you pregnant," he pleads loudly.

I bite the inside of my cheek to hold in my laugh. *Is he for real?*

Oh, God what must this look like? I am heavily pregnant. I roll my lips as I try to play along.

"I'm your wife's personal assistant for God's sake. She's going to find out eventually."

The ladies behind us all gasp.

Cameron drops his head and scrunches his eyes shut. "All those times in the storeroom at her office should never have happened," he replies coldly. "I knew it was wrong, but I just couldn't stop coming back. Even tonight, we shouldn't have had sex again. You're like a drug. A beautiful, fuckable drug."

Our eyes linger on each other's and I feel my heart flutter in my chest.

Even when lying he still does it for me.

"Leave her for me," I beg. "I'll do anything. Please."

He bites his bottom lip hard and his brow furrows. "I can't, she's pregnant with twins and due the same week as you, you know that. You went to her baby shower and she named you the godmother. I can't help it if my sperm is super potent."

I bite down on my bottom lip to stop myself from laughing. "But I love you," I cry.

"You love my dick; don't worry, you can always have that," he offers.

"Why, you fucking asshole!" the lady behind us growls as she hits him in the back of the head with an open hand.

I burst out laughing, and Cameron ducks for cover as she continues her assault. "How." *Smack.* "Dare." *Smack.* "You." *Smack.* "Treat her this way." *Smack, smack, smack.*

"Stop hitting me!" Cameron cries.

The man in the elevator is shocked, and I'm holding my stomach and bent over laughing.

"You good-looking men need to be taught a lesson," she growls as she smacks him hard again. "You're all out-of-control assholes."

The door opens, and Cameron runs out. I'm still bent over laughing with my hands on my knees. The lady, Cameron's attacker, says to me, "Do you need a lift anywhere, dear?"

I laugh. "No, thank you so much. It's okay."

Cameron comes back to me and takes my hand and I stand up.

The woman glares at him.

"It's all right. He's my husband," I stammer as I try to explain. "We were just joking around." I scrunch up my shoulders as I realize how ridiculous that must sound. "Sorry."

The three ladies' faces fall, and they exchange looks. "Just joking around?" she murmurs, horrified.

Cameron and I both nod. "Sorry." Cameron winces. He holds up his hand to show her his wedding ring. "It's just this weird thing we do. We lie in elevators so that other people hear us. My baby, my wife." He rubs my stomach. "Very happily my baby, four weeks to go. No other woman...I promise."

The lady looks at us blankly. "Well, that poor baby, having you two nut jobs for parents."

My face goes red and I giggle like a school girl. "Thanks for defending me," I offer.

She looks me up and down. "Good luck having his kid. You two are as stupid as each other." She and her friends storm through the lobby. "I've never heard of a more ridiculous hobby in all of my life!" she calls in a fluster over her shoulder.

Cameron watches her as she disappears. "We're going to see that woman on *America's Most Wanted* soon." He raises his eyebrows. "She's damn violent!"

I laugh again. "And you're an idiot."

———

Half an hour later I stand at the end of our bed as Cameron undresses me. It's darkened, with only the lamp light surrounding us.

I never had someone make love to me in my first pregnancy, and this deeper level of intimacy has me addicted.

He slowly slides my dress down and I hold onto his shoulders as I carefully step out of it. He stands to take my lips in his.

We kiss, soft and tender, and I can feel his erection through his pants as I slide my hand over his crotch.

He reaches around and undoes my bra, cupping my full breast in his hand as he dusts his thumb back and forth over my nipple.

"How you feeling, Bloss?" he whispers against my neck.

I smile as my eyes close. "That's code for *can I have sex with you?*" He tries his hardest to be gentle...although, in the throes of passion, we both fail miserably.

"I feel great," I whisper. "Ready for my man."

"Hmm." He nips my neck as his arousal notches up to a new level, and he slides my panties down my legs and bends to kiss my stomach tenderly.

He holds my hand as he lays me down, and then I watch in slow motion as he undoes his shirt. I'm blessed with the sight of his broad muscular torso, a scattering of dark hair, and that beautiful ripped abdomen.

With his dark eyes holding mine he slowly slides down his zipper, and pulls his pants and briefs down and takes them off. His dark hair falls just over his eyes and his lips are perfectly plump.

My insides begin to throb.

He's just so fucking beautiful—inside and out.

He lays beside me and we kiss for a long time, gentle, slow, and unhurried, and if this pregnancy has taught me anything, it's that Cameron Stanton makes love better than he fucks.

I never thought that would be possible.

His hands roam from my behind, up to my jaw, down over my breasts, and to my stomach.

I smile against his lips. I now know what it feels like to be worshipped.

*My body is his temple.*

God, some nights we can't stop. It's as if because we don't go as hard as we normally do that we can't quite put out the fire completely. It's a slow, hot, wet burn...one that we can do for an extended time.

I'm on my hormonal arousal peak and he's happily making sure my every whim is taken care of. He turns me onto my side and rustles around behind me. He then lifts my top leg over his forearm as he slowly slides his body into mine.

My breath catches.

My eyes close in pleasure and my head falls back to his shoulder.

He goes slowly, in and out, and deeper and deeper, and God this feels... so fucking good.

With his hand protectively on my pregnant stomach, his lips on my neck and his body slowly pumping into mine, I have a new kind of happiness.

It's called perfection.

———

The bathroom light wakes me, and I roll over; it feels like I only just got to sleep. Cam is up and showered and getting dressed for the day. He walks back into the room and smiles when he sees me. "Sorry, babe, did I wake you?"

"No," I sigh.

He sits on the side of the bed and pushes my hair back from my forehead. "You okay?" He bends and kisses me softly. "You tossed and turned all night."

"Yeah, I'm fine," I mumble. "Just can't get comfortable." I glance over at the clock. "You're up early," I notice.

"Yeah." He stands and grabs his shoes. "I have a quadruple bypass on today."

I fake a smile as I watch him. I can't even imagine the amount of pressure he's under every day at work.

People's lives are literally in his hands.

"It's going to be a long day." He continues putting his shoes on. "Adrian is on standby if you need anything, okay?"

"I'm not going to need anything, Cam." I roll onto my side

toward him. "I still have four weeks to go."

"Yeah, well, until Jameson comes back from vacation on Monday, you just take it easy please."

I smile. Cameron is obsessed with not missing the labor. He already missed his first child being born. Until the last few weeks when he's been so jumpy, I never knew how much it really affected him.

"You have my word. I'm not going into labor until Jameson comes home from Tahiti," I promise. "I went overdue with Owen. We have heaps of time."

He stands and watches me for a while. "Murph is coming over to take you out to lunch."

I smile sleepily. "You to mean to check on me?"

"That, too," he mutters dryly.

"Go to work, Dr. Stanton." I wave with my fingertips. "Go save a life."

He kisses me softly. "Bye, Bloss," he whispers. "I love you."

"Hmm." I sigh sleepily as I run my fingers through his stubble, hmm...he smells good. "Love you, too."

Owen patters into the room. "Dad."

"Hey, buddy." Cam smiles softly as he pulls his son into a hug. "Get into bed with Momma."

He pulls back the blankets and Owen crawls in sleepily. Cameron tucks him in and Owen snuggles into me and I kiss his little head. Although Owen's night visits are far less frequent, they still happen sometimes.

I think Cameron actually prefers him to sleep with us. He tears those blankets back so quick when he sees Owie, it's almost laughable.

With one last look he leaves the room, and I fall back into my uncomfortable slumber with two little arms cuddling my back.

---

"Come on, Owie, grab your school bag," I call from the bottom of the stairs.

I hold my stomach and wince. Fuck's sake...I'm so uncomfortable.

This baby has moved into the most sadistic position possible...right on my spine.

I push one side of my stomach, hoping to move it. I say *it* because we have no idea what *it* is. We don't know the sex of the baby yet, as we both wanted a surprise.

Owen smiles as he comes down the stairs, and he pats my stomach as he walks past me. He doesn't really talk to me much anymore, he talks to my stomach. He's so excited about being a big brother.

Between Cam and Owen, this baby is going to be spoiled rotten. We make our way to the school and I sit in the car in the drop-off lane. "I might not walk you in today, Owie." I rub my stomach. "My back is a little bit sore."

"That's okay, Mom." He leans over and kisses my cheek.

"Have a nice day." I smile

"Okay." He jumps out of the car and runs past the school's front gates with his back pack on.

My stomach tightens and then releases. Oww! What was that?

An uneasy feeling sweeps over me. "It's not." I talk out loud to myself. I blow out a breath and pull back into the traffic.

Imagine if it was labor? Cam can't leave surgery because he doesn't have any backup,

No...it's not...don't worry...it's way too early for that.

I get home and decide to have a shower. I undress, and as

I'm stepping in it happens again. I frown as my stomach tightens and then releases a few seconds later.

It's not painful... what is it?

Braxton Hicks... yes... of course.

It's just Braxton Hicks.

My body is getting ready for labor, that's all. I smile as I stand under the hot water and it feels so relaxing on my sore back, I might even go back to bed once I get out.

For nearly an hour I stand under the water, simply because I have nowhere to be and it feels so good not having to rush around. I don't think I have ever had a not- rushed shower since I started med school seven years ago.

My stomach has been tightening and relaxing, but it's not painful at all, so I know it's not labor... just Braxton Hicks.

I hop out of the shower and get dressed and lie on the bed. I really do feel out of sorts today.

I am woken by the house phone ringing and I frown. That's weird, nobody ever calls the house phone. I scramble over to the bedside table and answer.

"Hello?"

"Oh, my God. Where have you been?" Adrian demands.

"What?"

"I've been trying to call you for half an hour; I was beginning to panic."

I roll over; my stomach clenches and it hurts. I screw up my face.

Fuck.

"What's wrong?" I frown as I rub my hand over my stomach.

*Not today, baby...Daddy's not here.*

"Where do you want to go for lunch?" Adrian asks. "I'm going to book somewhere now."

"Do you just want to pick something up and we can eat here?"

"Oh, okay." He pauses for a moment. "Are you all right?"

I close my eyes and I know I'm worrying for nothing. "Just a bit of a sore back. Being a whale will do that to you," I joke.

"Oh." He thinks for a moment. "All right, see you soon."

I slowly get up and walk around the room.

Okay, even if this is early stages of labor, which it's not... but if it is...

Cameron will be finished in surgery by the time the baby comes anyway. I glance at the clock.

**11am.**

Shit, his big surgeries normally take at least twelve hours, and he would have started at 7am... so we're looking at either eight or nine o'clock tonight before he's out.

I take out my phone and type a ridiculous question that I already know the answer to.

How to slow down labor

I wait for the answers to appear.

Empty your bladder. Lie down tilted towards your left side; this may slow down or stop signs and symptoms. Avoid lying flat on your back; this may cause contractions to increase. Drink several glasses of water, because dehydration can cause contractions.

---

Ok, I lie down on my left side and try to calm down. I'm not even in labor. I'm just being silly, I know that. Stop being over-dramatic.

I Google again.

---

The latent phase can last several days or weeks before active labor starts. Some women can feel backache or cramps during this phase. Some women have bouts of contractions lasting a few hours, which then stop and start up again the next day. This is normal.

---

Oh good, this is normal. Great. See, nothing to worry about. I search again, and frown.

---

Preterm labor is labor that happens too early, before 37 weeks of pregnancy. If you have preterm labor, your health care provider may recommend some treatments that may help stop your contractions and prevent health problems in you and your baby. These treatments are not a guarantee to stop preterm labor.

---

Fuck. I search.

---

Problems for baby born at 36 weeks' gestation.

---

The answer comes back.

---

At 36 weeks, the risk of health complications decreases significantly.
    The risk is much lower from babies
    born even at 35 weeks.
    But late preterm babies are still at risk for:

Respiratory Distress
    Jaundice
    Low Birth weight
    NICU Admission
    Developmental Delays/Special Needs
    Patent Ductus arteriosus
    By far, RDS is the biggest risk for babies born at 36 weeks. Baby boys seem to have more trouble than infant girls.

---

Fuck... calm down... it's not happening. But if I do go into active labor, I need to get to the hospital as soon as I can so that they can try to stop it.

Yes. Okay, that's the plan.

My stomach clenches again and I screw up my face and rub my stomach.

"Stay in there and be a good baby, please?" I whisper. "Not today. You're not cooked yet."

For an hour I lie on my side as my stomach clenches and tightens. Nothing else has happened so I'm just going to wait to see. If I go to the hospital too early they'll just send me home.

My phone rings, it's Adrian. "Hello?" I answer.

"Do you want a coffee or something?"

"Can you just come now, please?" I ask.

"What's up?" He sounds like he's frowning.

"I think I'm having contractions but I'm not sure. If I am, we have to get to the hospital as quickly as possible," I blurt out in a rush.

The line stays silent.

"Adrian?" I ask.

"I'm here," he murmurs. "Just having a silent panic attack."

"You and me both."

"On my way, baby." He hangs up.

I lie down and try to calm myself some more, and twenty minutes later I hear Adrian's Corvette roar up the driveway and the door slam with force. Then I hear his voice. "Ashley! Where are you?" he calls.

"Up here," I call back.

He takes the stairs two at a time and comes running into the bedroom. "Oh, my God, what's going on?"

I smile, and he comes and sits next to me on the bed and takes my hand in his. "Are you all right?" he pants.

I giggle. "A lot calmer than you seem. Did you just get a speeding ticket on the way here?"

He widens his eyes. "Like I care?" He shakes his head and rubs my stomach. "What happened?"

I shrug. "I'm probably being overdramatic." I pause. "I've just been having back pain since last night, and now my stomach has started to contract."

He frowns as he listens.

"And I Googled it; if I'm in labor I need to get to the hospital to try to slow it down a little."

Adrian's eyes widen in horror. "You're a doctor, Ashley. How do you not know if you're in labor?"

"Because I'm not in pain," I snap. "I'm uncomfortable."

"Oh. Right." He bites his bottom lip as he thinks for a moment. "Well, let's call the hospital and see what they say."

I nod. "All right."

He Googles the number on his phone. "Do you want to speak?"

"Yes." I hold my hand out for the phone and he passes it to me.

It rings. "Hello, can I have the maternity ward please?" I ask.

"Sure, transferring you now."

It rings again. "Hello, maternity ward."

"Hello, this is Ashley Tucker."

"Hi, Ashley," the nurse replies.

I scrunch up my face. "I'm probably being a drama queen, but I've been having Braxton Hicks for two hours now."

"How far are you, Ashley?"

"Thirty-six weeks."

"Okay. Any showing or broken water?"

I shake my head. "No."

"All right then. Can you come in, so we can see what's going on?"

I nod. "Okay." I pause. "Do you think I'm in labor?"

"Probably not, dear. Don't worry. As long as your water doesn't break, everything will be fine."

I smile and nod. "All right, I'm on my way."

I pass the phone back to Adrian. "What did they say?" He frowns.

"As long as my water doesn't break, it's all good."

He puts his hand on his chest. "Oh, thank God." He grabs my hand and pulls me off the bed and I waddle into the bathroom I feel the urge to go and then *bam*.

I feel a sharp pop.

My water breaks... all over the floor... like, flooded.

My eyes widen. "Fuck! Adrian!" I call.

"What?" he calls.

"My water broke!"

"What?" he shrieks. He comes running into the bathroom and his face falls in horror when he sees how much there is. He puts both hands over his mouth before he regains his composure. "This is fine," he speaks calmly. "This is all fine." He takes out his phone and starts to dial a number.

I laugh; the look of sheer terror on his face is priceless. "Who are you calling?" I ask.

"Cameron," he snaps. He starts to pace with his hand in his suit pocket.

"Cameron is in surgery." I shake my head. "He's going to be hours."

His face falls.

"Let me call him." I pick up my phone and dial his PA's number. She answers on the first ring. "Hi, Ash!" she greets.

I screw up my face because I really don't want to say this out loud. "We have a problem."

"What's that?" she murmurs.

"My water has broken."

"Oh. Fuck!" she replies.

I smile; I've never heard her swear before.

"How long do you think he's going to be?" I ask.

"Oh God, Ash." She hesitates. "I'll put him on the phone." I hear her walking into the surgery; she sits at the nurses' station at the back of his operating theatre. The phone goes silent; she must have covered the phone with her hand.

Moments later. "Hey, Bloss," Cameron answers calmly. "You're on speaker, babe," he reminds me. I close my eyes. That means that the ten people in surgery can all hear what he's saying but his hands are tied up doing the operation and he can't hold the phone.

"Cam." I screw up my face. "I just called to tell you that my water has broken and I'm with Adrian and we're on our way to hospital."

"Fuck," he growls.

"How far apart are the contractions?" he asks calmly.

"That's the thing, I don't think I'm in active labor yet. It's all right, no need to panic."

"No pain?" he questions.

"Just back pain."

"How long have you been having back pain?"

"All night." My eyes widen. "That's not..." My voice trails off. Don't tell me I've been in labor since last night.

"Ash?" Cam asks.

"I'm just going to get to the hospital, and I'll call you back, all right?" I try to comfort him.

"Oh my God," he replies. "Drive carefully, please."

"How long do you think you'll be in surgery for, Cam?" I hate to ask but I need to know.

"At least two hours," he replies.

I close my eyes and I can almost hear his heart rate rise through the phone.

"It's okay, it's going to be a lot longer than that," I reassure him.

"Just get here safely. Put Adrian on the phone," he asks.

I pass Adrian the phone and I go and get changed and put a pad in, as I'm still leaking amniotic fluid.

*Fucking hell.*

"Yes." I hear Adrian answer. "Yes, I know," he replies. "Cameron. I fucking know that." Adrian snaps. "Yes, I know!"

He listens for a moment. "Just hurry up and finish your operation, will you!" Adrian demands.

I smile; Adrian has no idea he's on speaker. These two always scream at each other when they get stressed out. I get an image of all of Cameron's interns and the nurses listening and what they must be thinking.

"Fine," Adrian snaps. "Yes! I know!" he yells.

I walk out of the bathroom to see Adrian roll his eyes, his hand on his hip as he listens to Cameron's lecture. He exhales heavily. "See you soon." He hangs up and then quickly falls into role play and fakes a calm smile. "Ready to go, chick?"

"Yep." I grab my handbag.

He looks around. "Where's your hospital bag, Ash?" He frowns.

"God, I can't believe this." I shake my head because I'm forgetting everything.

I think for a moment. "Did Cameron remind you to get the hospital bag?"

He smirks. "Yes."

"What else did he tell you?" I frown because it seems I can't think without my husband doing it for me these days.

"To organize with Jenna to get Owen and to keep you calm."

I nod. "Right." I look at Adrian, who is now perspiring heavily. "We've got this, Adrian. We can do this without Cam if we have to." I grab my bag. "And we might."

Adrian looks like he's about to faint.

"I know," he murmurs.

Burning pain rips through my stomach, and I bend over and hold my stomach.

"What's happening?" Adrian cries.

"Contraction," I murmur. "Oh, that's a real one." I wince.

My stomach clenches hard and the pain is strong. "We need to get to the hospital, Adrian...and quick."

"Quick?" he stammers with wide eyes. "How quick?"

"That wasn't a first contraction."

He looks at me blankly, not understanding.

"That was a 'things are moving faster than I would like to' contraction."

Adrian puts his hands on his head. "What do I do?"

"Get me to the hospital."


## Cameron

I close my eyes and try to control my erratic heartbeat. Midway through a major heart operation is not the time to lose my cool.

Everyone in the room has fallen silent, as if scared to speak.

"Hanna," I call.

"Yes, Doctor?"

Hanna is one of my PAs. "Can you get Peter Martin on the phone, please?"

"Yes, of course."

Peter is a heart surgeon who works in the other hospitals in L.A.

I keep working.

Hanna comes back to me. "Peter Martin is in a conference in London."

I close my eyes. "Get Hamish on the line, please."

Hamish is a colleague who runs the country side of our practice.

"Yes, Doctor." She disappears again, and I continue my surgery.

"He's on the line, Doctor," Hanna calls, and puts him onto speaker.

"Hello," I say.

"Hey fuck knuckle," he calls in his boisterous voice.

"I'm in surgery, Hamish, and you're on speaker," I snap.

Everyone laughs.

"Oops, sorry everyone," he calls.

I roll my eyes. "I've got a problem."

"What's up?"

"Ashley's in labor and I'm in the middle of a bypass."

"Oh shit," he replies. "That is a problem."

"Can you get down here?"

"I'm fully booked this afternoon."

"Cancel your appointments."

He stays silent.

I bite my bottom lip. "I'll finish the surgery, but I just need someone here in case something happens."

He thinks for a moment. "Yes. Okay. I'll be there in two hours."

"Two hours?" I snap.

"That's how long it takes to drive there."

"Get on a plane. I'll hire you a private plane," I stammer.

"It will take that long getting into one airport and out of the other...it's quicker if I drive."

*Shit.*

"All right." I pause for a moment. "Can you leave immediately?"

"Yes." He sighs. "On my way."

I blow out a breath and the nurse wipes the perspiration from my brow. The room falls silent and everyone is edgy. I inhale deeply as I try to calm myself down. "Hanna," I call.

"Yes, Doctor."

"Can you keep in contact with Ashley by phone, please, and let me know if there's any change, other than that I need to concentrate here."

"Yes, of course." She pauses for a moment. "Calling her now."

I inhale again as I try to slow my heart to a regular beat.

It's okay, I'm going to get there... fate couldn't be so cruel as to let me miss another birth.

*Hold on, Bloss... hold on.*

## Ashley

"Ahhhhh!" I call as I sit slumped over in the car.

Adrian's eyes are nearly popping from the sockets and he's driving like a maniac. We've been stuck in traffic for forty-five minutes. "It's okay, Ash. It's okay." He tries to soothe me.

"It's not fucking okay!" I yell.

He shakes his head as he grips the steering wheel with white-knuckle force and changes lanes aggressively. The car behind honks its horn, and he flips them the bird.

"Oh, just great, get us killed by a road rager, why don't you?" I stammer.

"I'd like to see someone pull something right now." He changes lanes again. "I could totally take them if my adrenaline level has anything to do with it."

I laugh as my contraction subsides, and I put my head back on the seat.

We drive for a moment in silence. "Okay, tell me about panting," he asks.

"I don't know." I shake my head. "Controls your pain, apparently."

His eyes flick between me and the road. "Well, we need to pant. How do you do it? Show me."

I blow out in short quick successions, and show him what they teach you in prenatal classes.

"Like this?" He practices, and I burst out laughing.

"Yes. Like that." I wince. "Oh, here comes another one!" I call.

Adrian's eyes widen in fear and he starts to pant.

I laugh as I screw up my face in pain. "You look fucking ridiculous."

"Do it with me, Ash!" he cries, blowing in an overexaggerated fashion toward the steering wheel.

We both pant as he drives like a maniac, and eventually it subsides.

"See, that was better." He smiles a proud of himself smile.

I lay my head back against the seat as I breathe heavily. "I hope Cam makes it." I smile sadly over at him. He takes my hand in his sympathetically and picks it up and kisses the back of it. "It's all right if he doesn't—You've got me."

I smile.

Jenna is in New York and Tash is at Willowvale. "Can you ring Tash?" I ask.

"Yes, sure." He hits her number on the car Bluetooth.

"Hey, babe," she answers.

"Hi, Tash," I call.

"Ash? What's wrong?" she snaps.

"She's in labor," Adrian calls. "Get your ass to L.A!"

"Oh, my God. It's too early." She shrieks. "Where's Cameron?"

"He's in surgery."

"Oh, shit," she murmurs. "Joshua!" she calls. "Ashley's in labor."

"Tash, can you ring Jenna and organize Owen to get picked up from school, please?" Adrian asks. "This is quite unexpected and a bit crazy on this end."

"Ahhh!" I cry as another contraction rips through me.

Adrian starts to pant as his eyes flick between me and the road. "Pant, pant, pant!" he cries.

Natasha bursts out laughing. "Oh, please tell me there's a camera in the car."

"See you soon," Adrian calls and then he hangs up on her, annoyed at her finding this funny.

I smile as I lay back against the seat. "You do have to admit this is pretty funny."

He looks at me deadpan as he grips the steering wheel. "Hilarious."

We pull up to the hospital and he jumps out of the car. "Can somebody help us please while I park the car?" he calls to a passing nurse.

"Of course," she calls. She quickly returns with a wheelchair and Adrian helps me out of his low car and into the wheelchair.

"Let me guess," the nurse quips, all smiles. "Maternity?"

"Yes," Adrian snaps. "I'm just parking the car, Ash."

"Okay." I smile.

"I'll take her up," the nurse replies.

We make our way up to the maternity ward and the nurses help me and take me into a room and onto a bed. They instantly put the baby monitor on my stomach and we all start to watch it.

"I'm only thirty-six weeks. It can't come yet," I whisper through fear.

"Thirty-six weeks is fine, Ashley, you know that."

"Are you here alone?" another nurse asks.

"Cameron is in surgery," I reply sadly. "Can we just slow it down, so he can make it?"

The nurses both smile sympathetically.

Adrian comes sprinting down the hall at full speed and runs straight past the room.

"Excuse me, sir!" a nurse calls. "Where are you running to?"

"Oh." *Pants.* "Ashley." *Pants.* "Stanton."

"In here, Adrian!" I call.

I screw up my face as another contraction comes, and watch the monitor.

"Oh." The nurse smiles as her eyes stay glued to the monitor. "That's a big one. I think we need to take a look at what's going on."

I ride the contraction out, then she takes my pants off and I glance over at Adrian. He points to the door with his thumb.

"You're not going anywhere!" I snap.

She spreads my legs and the blood starts to drain from Adrian's face.

"Come up this end," the nurse comforts.

"He's not very good with vaginas," I pant.

The nurse smirks. "I thought as much."

She inspects me. "How long did you say your husband is going to be, Ash?"

"I'm not sure. Why?" I frown.

"You're eight centimeters dilated, darling. Baby will be here very soon."

I look at her and then over to Adrian. He's a pale shade of green.

I swallow the lump in my throat. "Call Cam."

He dials his number. "Hello, Hanna, this is Adrian. We need to speak to Cameron please," he asks.

"What's going on?" Cam replies.

"She's eight centimeters dilated," Adrian replies. "You need to get here. Now!"

"I'm nearly finished, my back-up surgeon has just arrived. I'm twenty minutes away." He pauses. "Put Ash on."

"Hello."

"Hey, Bloss," he says gently.

I smile down the phone; just hearing his voice makes me teary.

"You all right, baby?"

I nod through my tears.

"Yep," is all I can push out.

"Hold on, sweetheart, I'm coming."

I nod and scrunch my eyes shut as another contraction comes. My doctor walks into the room. "The doctor is here."

"Put him on," Cameron asks.

I hand the phone to the doctor. "It's Cameron."

He frowns and takes the phone. "Hello?" He listens for a moment. "Why? Where are you?" he asks. "Just a minute. "He puts the phone down and gives me an internal and then gets back on the phone. "She's nearly ready to push. I'll do my best. It's progressing very fast." He hands the phone back to me.

"Hey, Bloss. I'm coming, babe."

I nod as tears start to roll down my face. He's not going to make it. I know he's not.

"I love you," I whisper.

"I love you, too. I'll be there as soon as I can." He hangs up.

I start to cry, blubbering-mess-crying, and I just want Cameron here. Why, oh, why today of all days?

My eyes widen, and then I scrunch them shut.

"What is it?" Adrian frowns.

"I need to push."

## Cameron

I tear off my gloves and run out of the operating room. I bang the elevator button three times.

"Come on, come on." I watch in slow motion, my foot tapping fast. "Please, please let me make it," I whisper under my breath. The door opens, and I run in and bang the close-door button.

Level four: Maternity.

The ride up to level four is the slowest I've ever seen. It finally opens onto the floor and I run down the hall to the delivery suite and burst through the doors.

"Where is she?" I cry.

"Birthing suite two, on the left."

I run down and run into the room in time to see my beautiful Ashley in bed, her face screwed up in pain as she tries to hold off. "I'm here, Ash!" I cry.

She looks up at me through her tears; her hair is wet with perspiration and she's panting. I've never seen someone so beautiful.

"Oh, baby," I whisper as I rush to her and brush her hair back from her forehead.

I smile as I kiss her lips, and she clings to me as if her life depends on it.

"Next contraction, Ashley, I want you to push," the doctor directs.

I kiss her softly. "You can do this."

She nods as she screws her face up.

I hold her leg back as I brace myself. "Get ready, Bloss."

"I'm going to go," Adrian murmurs.

"Don't you dare go anywhere!" Ashley screams.

"Really?" he whispers. He goes to the back wall and stands silently, as if scared to move.

With a nurse holding one of her legs and me holding the other the contraction comes, and she pushes as hard as she can. My eyes widen as I see the head. The contraction stops and the baby's head pops back in.

"You can do this, Ash, come on," I urge.

She nods as she psyches herself up again. The contraction comes and she pushes as hard as she can. Her face turns bright red and she cries out in pain.

"I can see it, so close," I whisper. "Come on, Bloss, come on."

She gives a big push and the head is out.

She pants, and I smile broadly. "One more, one more," I chant as she grips my hand with white-knuckle force.

She pushes again and screams as the baby slides out.

Blood and mucus and... silence.

I hold my breath; the nurse picks up the baby and rubs it with a towel, and finally it begins to scream.

"Oh, thank God!" Ashley cries.

"It's a girl," the doctor announces.

I cut the umbilical cord and the doctor goes to pass her to Ash.

"Pass her to her father first, please," Ashley says.

My eyes search hers as my heart freefalls from my chest.

The doctor passes her to me, and I stare at her.

Shocked. Shocked that I nearly didn't make it. Shocked that I did.

Shocked that we made this beautiful little person.

She's so perfect, and she looks up at me as she tries to focus her eyes.

I blink so I can see her through the tears, and I take her to

Ash and bend down and kiss my beautiful wife. We hold each other over our little girl.

"You did it. I love you. I love you," I whisper.

"I love you, too," she sobs.

"What are you naming her?" the nurse asks.

Our eyes meet, and she smiles and nods.

"Sophia Anne Stanton," I whisper.

Ashley smiles against my lips as we kiss.

"Owen's here." Adrian says, smiling.

"Can you get him please?" Ashley asks.

Adrian disappears, and the nurse cleans Ash up. Minutes later, he returns with Owen. "Owie, come and meet your baby sister." I pick him up and he stares at her, unsure what to say.

"Isn't she beautiful?" I whisper in wonder.

He smiles broadly and sticks his little tongue out, as if pleased with himself. The nurse holds the baby to Ash's breast and she slowly starts to suck. I smile softly.

I've never seen anything more beautiful; emotion overwhelms me, and I tear up again.

"What's she doing?" Owen frowns.

"She's drinking," I whisper. "That's how babies drink milk."

Owen's face falls in horror. "Well, yuck!" He frowns. "That's just disgusting!"

The room breaks into laughter and I shake my head.

Only Owen.

## Ashley- Nine years later

I stand at the kitchen window as I watch Cam. He's out in the garden with the kids, chasing them with water balloons.

They're hiding, although Owen is sitting on the deckchair, watching as he chats on his phone to his little girlfriend.

We have five children—six including Cameron. He's still a big kid and nothing has changed at all.

Owen is fifteen, Sophia in nine, Zander is seven, Spencer is five, and Juliet is eighteen months. I thought watching Cameron with Owen was heart-melting; you should see him with five of them.

We're at Pemberley and, funnily enough, this is now Cameron's favorite place in the world. We've added to the house and still live permanently in L.A. It's getting increasingly harder to get to Pemberley now that Owen is older and has a social life.

One day, Cam and I will live here permanently. I wish our children could stay at this age forever. Joshua and Natasha's children are in their late teens now and are giving them a run for their money, wild as all hell. They moved back to LA permanently and the kids have all began to work for Joshua in his office. Apparently they are sending Adrian and Joshua grey. All of the men in the office are after Jordana and Blake is chasing after everything in a skirt. Cameron and I think it's hilarious... because it's not us. I dread when our turn comes.

Cameron looks up and spots me watching him through the window, and he smiles sexily and makes his way across the garden. Before I know it he wraps his arms around me from behind and kisses me.

"Et si on filait au lit."

*Translation: Let's sneak off to bed.*

He nibbles on my neck and I smile as I try to wriggle away from him.

"No." I turn, and he takes me in his arms. I look up at him and he kisses me softly. "You know, you're kind of all right for a farm boy." My hands drop to his behind and I give it a squeeze.

Everything is still gorgeous about my man; he's only gotten better with age.

He smiles sexily down at me. "I'll show you what a farm boy can really do."

"Dad!" Juliet calls.

He rolls his eyes.

"Dad!" Zander yells. "Where did you go?"

He puffs air in his cheeks and looks out the window, and then smiles broadly as an idea comes to him. He ducks down and crawls through the kitchen and back through the house.

"What are you doing?" I ask as he crawls up the hall, towards the front door.

"I'm going to attack from the front. You were just my prop."

I smirk. "Thanks a lot."

"You're welcome. Anytime," he replies.

I watch through the window as he sneaks around the side of the house and starts running toward them and throwing water bombs from nowhere. The kids all scream and run.

His beautiful wild laugh echoes throughout the farm.

Life is good.

I'm the luckiest girl in the world.


**The End.**


*Read on for an excerpt of Marx Girl,*
*the next book in this series.*

# MARX GIRL EXCERPT
## AVAILABLE NOW

**Bridget**

"Don't look at me like you want me... not if you don't," I murmur into the silence.

He sits back and readjusts himself in his pants. His dark eyes hold mine, yet he doesn't answer me.

The water laps around me as I lie on the inflatable mattress, floating around the pool in my white string bikini. The sun is just setting, and everyone has disappeared to get ready for dinner.

We're alone.

His eyes are locked on me from his poolside deckchair position.

He has no right to look at me, to watch me with wanting eyes.

But he does.

And I still like it.

Ben is my sister's family's bodyguard and the head of their security.

Things are difficult between us, to say the least.

The attraction between us wasn't supposed to happen, but forbidden had never felt so good.

Six-foot-three-inches tall with sandy hair, honey-brown eyes, and a large, muscular physique, he's a by-product of being ex-military.

Ben Statham is one hell of a man.

From the lingering looks, the clenching deep in my sex when he looks at me, the smouldering fire whenever he would sneak into my room late at night...

It led to our story beginning six months ago, when my sister Natasha became involved with her then-boyfriend, Joshua Stanton.

I was always with Tash, and Ben was always with Josh. We came together through circumstance. Acquaintances and nothing more.

He was the strong man at the back of the crowd, watching over everyone.

I was busy watching him.

The rest of the world was concentrating on my beloved sister and Joshua's blossoming relationship.

I was concentrating on fighting the attraction, but the pull to him only grew day by day.

Laughter turned to conversation, conversation introduced lingering looks, and lingering looks turned to goose bumps, until one day in the kitchen pantry it happened.

Ben kissed me.

It was the most perfect kiss I've ever had.

It was sweet, sexy, and it opened a world of passion I never even knew existed.

For three weeks we snuck a kiss in where we could until, in a moment of foggy passion, I asked him to come to my room after everyone went to sleep that night. He did.

We made love. Storybook love.

The perfection we'd created carried on for six weeks, until tragedy struck our family. As the head of security Ben blamed himself, and pulled away from me.

When I needed him the most, he was nowhere around to offer support.

We've hardly spoken since.

And now we're here on a family vacation in Kamala, Thailand.

My feelings for him haven't changed.

He's still the head of security.

I'm still his boss' sister-in-law.

But he left me when I needed him the most, and I won't forget that anytime soon.

Our eyes are locked.

"Why would you think I don't want you?" he whispers in his heavy South African accent.

I frown, unsure how to answer. Eventually, I reply, "Do you?"

He sips his beer, contemplating the right way to answer.

I run my fingers through the water beneath me as I try to articulate my thoughts.

I don't know what's going on with us, but I do know I can't stand feeling the way I feel.

I can't go on without him giving me the answers I need. He's a strong man who doesn't show his true feelings, but what happened to us? How do you go from passionate lovers to being nothing, without even a conversation?

There was no fight, no discussion. Just silence.

He doesn't answer my question. His jaw clenches as his gaze holds mine. My eyes search his.

What the fuck is going on with him?

Does he want me to beg?

*Answer me, damn it.*

I climb off the inflatable mattress and make my way to the pool steps. I want to be the one who ends the conversation, not the other way around.

Who am I kidding?

I'm the only one in this conversation. I slowly walk out of the pool, and his hungry gaze drops down my body. I bend and pick up my towel to wrap it around my waist, and with one last lingering look I walk inside.

His refusal to address our issues infuriates me.

It hurts me, and it makes me wonder if everything we shared was an illusion.

I know he's strong. I know he's not a talker. But those nights in his arms were filled with tenderness and love.

Where is *that* man?

Because I want him back.

I lie in the darkness at 1:00 a.m. The sound of the ocean drifts through the room, and a soft breeze rolls over my body. As usual, I'm torturing myself with thoughts of Ben Statham and his beautiful body. *Where is he now? Is he asleep?*

The last time we were together I told him I loved him. I never meant to, but I couldn't help it. I was all soft and emotional from my orgasm high, and the words just slipped out.

*Is that why he ran?*

I blow out a deep breath and stare at the ceiling as I go over that last night we spent together for the ten-thousandth time.

If I knew it was to be our last night together I would have done more, said more, done anything to make him stay.

The door opens, and I roll over. My heart catches in my chest.

"Ben," I whisper.

He walks in and closes the door behind him, his hands clenching at his sides. He seems nervous.

I frown into the diluted light as I watch him.

"I wanted to see you," he whispers.

I lie still. He can do the talking this time.

"I look at you like I want you..." He pauses and clenches his hands at his sides. "...because I do," he whispers.

I frown.

"You have no idea how badly I want you, Bridget, or how hard it is for me to stay away."

"Then why? Why are you doing this to us?" I whisper.

He sits on the side of the bed and cups my face in his hands, his eyes searching mine in the moonlit room as his thumb gently dusts over my bottom lip. He hesitates, and frowns as if pained. "I'm not who you think I am."

I sit up, resting on my elbow, and I frown as I watch him. "Are you married?" I whisper. Oh, no. My heart starts to hammer. He has a whole other life in South Africa, doesn't he? I have no idea what's going on at home for him.

He shakes his head, and a soft smile crosses his face. "No, I'm not married." He frowns harder, and leans in to kiss me softly. "But I'm not able to give you my heart." Tears fill my eyes.

He shakes his head. "Please..." He pauses. "Know that I love you,

Bridget."

"Ben," I whisper. "What's going on? Talk to me."

He leans in and sweeps his tongue gently between my lips, and I scrunch my face up to fight the tears.

It's there again, the urge to tell him that I love him.

This man makes me so weak.

I sit up and wrap my arms around his broad shoulders. We kiss slowly, and I feel my arousal start to rise.

"I've come to say goodbye," he whispers against my lips.

"What?" My eyes search his again. "But you said—"

He cuts me off. "I can't be who you want me to be, Bridget."

"Yes, you can, Ben. You're who I want," I whisper angrily. Damn it, I hate this sneaking around shit. I can't even raise my voice the way I want to.

He runs his thumb over my cheekbone as he studies my face. "I have a past, Didge, one that I don't want to ever catch up with you. I won't bring that into your life."

I shake my head. "What are you talking about? We all have a past. We can work it out together, Ben."

"Goodbye, Bridget," he whispers sadly before he tries to stand, but I grab his wrist.

"No. Don't go," I beg as I lose control. "Don't leave me. I love you."

He bends and kisses me gently. "Remember me with love, angel." I stare at him through my tears.

"I love you," he whispers.

I suddenly become panicked. "Don't go," I beg.

He stares at me in the darkness.

I shake my head, unable to stand it. I need more time. I need more time to try and make him stay. "One more time," I whisper. "Say goodbye to me properly."

"Bridget," he breathes.

"Ben, it's just the two of us here." I pull him down to kiss his lips softly. "If you want to say goodbye to me, do it when you have to. I can't bear to let you go tonight." My voice cracks in pain.

"Baby, *shh*." He calms me as he sweeps the hair back from my forehead and studies my face. "It will be all right."

"How can it be all right if you're leaving me?" I whisper through tears.

He takes me in his arms and we cling to each other tightly; so tight that it feels like I might break if I let him go. Maybe I will.

"I need you," I murmur against his lips as he kisses me. His tongue dances with mine as his hand roams over my hip and he squeezes it with force.

"Bridget," he murmurs, and I know that he's having an internal battle with himself.

He wants me, but he thinks this is the wrong thing to do.

But making love to Ben could never be wrong, and I'll face those consequences tomorrow. I slowly sit up and slide my white silk nightdress over my shoulders and throw it onto the floor. His eyes drop hungrily to my breasts. I lay back and spread my legs as a silent invitation. His eyes drop to the crotch of my pale pink panties.

His eyes darken and his tongue darts out to swipe over his bottom lip.

*Oh... he wants me all right.*

I run my hand up over my breast and squeeze it. "It's been six weeks since you've been inside me, Ben." I arch my back off the bed. "I can't stand another moment without you."

He frowns, and I see the last of his resistance teetering on the edge. "Fill me up, big boy. Make sure I never forget you."

His jaw clenches as his eyes flicker with arousal, and he stands in one quick movement to take his T-shirt off over his head.

My eyes roam over his thick, broad chest that's covered with a scattering of dark hair. His arms are huge, and I can see every muscle in his stomach. The distinct V of muscles that disappear into his jeans holds me captive. I drag my eyes to his perfect face, and my heart somersaults in my chest. He has the most beautiful body in the world... but it's his soul that I love. The dominant alpha man who has shown me what it's like to really love someone.

What it feels like to be adored and loved by someone so deeply that nothing else matters.

He knows what my body needs more than I do, and I wriggle on the bed as he slides his jeans down his legs. My mouth goes dry.

Holy fucking hell. He's a god.

His thick, hard cock hangs heavily between his legs, and he takes it in his hand to stroke it three times as his eyes hold mine.

"You want this, Bridget?" he whispers as he strokes himself.

I nod as my mouth goes dry, my eyes fixed on the pre-ejaculate that drips from the end. *Fuck, yeah.*

"You get over here and suck me. Make sure I never forget you."

Our eyes lock, and he gives me the best 'come fuck me' look I've ever seen.

Suddenly, I'm desperate. Desperate to please him.

Desperate to make him stay.

I scramble towards him on my knees and take him deep in my mouth. He inhales sharply.

"Good girl," he breathes as his hands fall to the back of my head.

My insides begin to melt, and I moan around him. He

pushes himself deep—so deep—and his eyes close in pleasure. I have to concentrate to block my gag reflex.

Fucking hell. Bringing him to his undoing is my favourite thing in the whole damn world.

He hisses as he builds a rhythm, my hair gripped tightly in his hands.

"Fuck, fuck, fuck," he murmurs under his breath.

"You like that, baby?" I whisper around him.

His eyes flicker with arousal. "I fucking... love that," he pants. A sheen of perspiration covers his skin and it revs me up even more.

He loses control and throws me onto the bed. I bounce high and then he's on me as he slides my panties down and throws them in the air, off the bed.

His lips trail down over my breasts, and he takes them into his mouth to suck them one at a time. His suction is so hard that my face scrunches up in pain and my back arches off the bed.

This is what he does to me.

He gets me so hot for him that I beg him to be rough, like I'm some kind of crazy animal beneath him that needs to be tamed.

Controlled.

His lips drop lower... and lower... and I hold my breath and close my eyes.

Oh, dear God, he's amazing at this.

*The king.*

His tongue sweeps through my flesh, and he grabs my legs and forces them back to the mattress. "Open up," he growls as his dark eyes hold mine. He tenderly kisses my inner thigh.

This is too much, too intense, too intimate. I look away.

"Watch me, Bridget," he commands.

I drag my eyes back to his.

"You watch my tongue lick up your cream and make this pretty little cunt dance." He licks his lips and sucks me again. The look of sheer pleasure on his face makes me blush.

I begin to convulse. For fuck's sake. How is one man so hot?

He bites my clitoris and I throw my head back and come in a rush.

Fuck's sake, I lasted two minutes.

He smiles as he licks me up, and then lifts one of my legs and then the other over his shoulders. In one sharp movement, Ben slams home deep.

"Ben!" I cry out.

"I got you, babe," he murmurs against my lips, and lies down on me.

Then he kisses me, and it's soft and tender and caring and... God.

This can't end. What we have is too good to ever end.

As if sensing my feelings, his face creases with pain against mine and he holds me that bit closer.

His body starts to ride mine. Long, slow, and deep. Our eyes are locked, and damn, this is the best sex I've ever had in my entire life.

Who am I kidding?

Every time with Ben is the best time of my life. The man is one hell of a lover.

Perspiration covers us as we drink each other in.

"Now..." he whispers, sensing his fast-approaching climax. "You need to come *now*." He picks up the pace and I clench around him.

He moans a guttural sound and buries his head deep into my neck, while I smile at the ceiling.

*You won't forget this in a hurry, big boy.*

His pumping gets harder and deeper, faster and faster, and I clench around him before I fall.

"Ahh..." I breathe.

I scrunch my eyes shut to stop the tears. He moans as he comes deep inside me.

We kiss, for a long time. It's soft and tender, and his body is still in mine, slowly emptying itself with slow pumps.

"I love you, Ben," I whisper.

"I love you, too," he breathes as he rests his head against my cheek. He pauses for a moment. "That's why I have to leave you." He pulls out of my body in one quick rush.

*What?* I sit up. *No.* "What are you talking about?" I whisper. "We can work it out."

His eyes search mine. "This is goodbye, Bridget; don't make this any harder than it already is."

"Ben..." I whisper. My body is still throbbing from the beating he just gave it.

He pulls on his clothes and I watch on in silence.

*Don't go. Please, don't go.*

With one last, lingering kiss, he stands and leaves my room without looking back.

I stare at the door after it closes behind him.

No. Please, God.

That didn't just happen.

Despair fills me.

I curl into a ball. My heart physically hurts in my chest, and I weep.

**To continue reading this story it is available now on Amazon.**

# AFTERWORD

**Thank you so much for reading.
You are making my dreams come true.**

Keep up to date with all the latest news
and online discussions by joining the Swan Squad VIP
Facebook group and discuss your favourite
books with other readers.
@tlswanauthor

Visit my website for updates and new release information.
www.tlswanauthor.com

# ABOUT THE AUTHOR

T L Swan is a Wall Street Journal, USA Today, and #1 Amazon Best Selling author. With millions of books sold, her titles are currently translated in twenty languages and have hit #1 on Amazon in the USA, UK, Canada, Australia and Germany. She is currently writing the screenplays for a number of her titles. Tee resides on the South Coast of NSW, Australia with her husband and their three children where she is living her own happy ever after with her first true love.

Made in the USA
Monee, IL
08 May 2024